"This is dangerous."

Connie looked around nervously as she spoke. Ken had gently pulled her down on the stack of Oriental carpets and his hands were lazily stroking her curves.

"I like living dangerously, don't you?" he said with a grin. He nuzzled her neck and started pushing her sweater up slowly.

"Well, we'll have to be really... careful... from here on out," Connie murmured, as she started to melt inside. "I don't want people finding out about us."

"Yes, we'll be careful," Ken whispered, his face still buried in her neck. Connie felt his warm breath caressing her ear. "But that doesn't mean we can't have fun...."

Bess Shannon has *always* been a writer, she says. Her love for writing and her talent for making up stories of her own at an early age were confirmed later on when she decided to pursue a career in advertising as a copywriter. She has also published several articles on advertising and marketing as well as a science fiction novel.

Her knowledge of the fierce competition between auction houses and museums and her fascination with Oriental art were the motivating factors for writing *Going, Going, Gone!*—an exciting addition to the Temptation line.

A New Yorker at heart, Bess knows all the endless marvels of Manhattan where she lives with her husband.

Going, Going, Gone!

BESS SHANNON

Harlequin Books

TORONTO • NEW YORK • LONDON
AMSTERDAM • PARIS • SYDNEY • HAMBURG
STOCKHOLM • ATHENS • TOKYO • MILAN

Published May 1990

ISBN 0-373-25398-2

Printed in U.S.A.

1

THE OBITUARY READ:

> NEW YORK, JANUARY 29TH. The Marquise de Vernay has died in her Manhattan residence at the age of ninety-seven. Born Augustine Carmody, of the Rochester family that built its fortune from streetcar and rail transportation, the Marquise was married three times. Her last husband, the Marquis Thierry, was of the noble French clan that traces its lineage directly to Charlemagne. He died in 1958.
>
> Although her wealth and titles would have guaranteed her a prominent place in international society, after a brilliant debut and marriage the Marquise became semireclusive. In later years she was considered somewhat eccentric. She was known to the public chiefly for her wide-ranging acquisitions of art and antiques—purchases in which price was no object.
>
> The collection of the Marquise de Vernay is known to include an outstanding selection of French Impressionists, furniture and fittings from the Palace of Versailles and the Doges Palace in Venice. Her holdings of both European and Asian

porcelains were described as "staggering" by one expert.

There were also persistent rumors that the Marquise had managed to acquire some of the jewels and furniture from the Winter Palace of the Russian czars, which fell out of sight under mysterious circumstances during the 1920s.

The Marquise leaves no direct descendants. Her only child was by her first husband, Wall Street swashbuckler Harry Cheney. Harry Cheney Jr. died in 1926 at the age of four.

Funeral plans for the Marquise are still incomplete.

"YOU'RE MAKING that noise again, Mom."

Constance Nathan lowered *The Times*. "What noise?"

"That *I want it* noise, kind of like Mrs. Wickes's cat makes when she sees birds through the window."

"Really? Well, Jeremy, I guarantee you people all over town—all over the world—are making that same noise."

"Why?"

"Because a very old lady has died who was very rich and owned tons and tons of beautiful things—things that the kind of people I work with will pay huge amounts of money to get. And I want to be in on it when they do. Be sure to finish your orange juice."

It was true. Constance could practically hear her competition and her customers making sounds of longing, greed, envy and ambition as they read the obituary. For decades the Vernay collection had been something like the Holy Grail to sellers and collectors of fine art. Everybody knew it existed, everybody wanted to find it, but nobody—except for the now late Marquise—knew just what it was.

"Is Veersbog going to sell this lady's things?"

"That's Villiers, Buck, dear. And yes," she agreed, her voice shifting into its firm determination mode, "we *will* be auctioning off the Vernay estate if I have anything to say about it." The professional side of Constance itched to grab the phone and start the whole process. But she'd sworn an ironclad oath to herself when she went back to work; business was to stay in the office, and home time—every minute of it—belonged to Jeremy.

She gazed fondly at her son whose seven-year-old face seemed to change from day to day. Today he was looking a little more like his father. Which reminded her, Bob had said he wanted to take Jeremy skating on their outing this weekend. Where, oh where in the apartment were his little skates? Would she and Bob have to conduct another inch-by-inch search of the boy's jam-packed room, as they did when his cap pistol vanished? Once again, she silently thanked her stars that she and her ex-husband had had the most amicable divorce possible.

Constance flicked her eyes to the kitchen clock and gasped. "Are you all ready for school, Jeremy?" But of course he wasn't, so she had to race to pack his bookbag and find his coat, hat and mittens before they grabbed a cab to his school in the East Nineties. A quick kiss on the school's front steps, then back in the cab where she finished her makeup.

It wasn't yet 8:15 at V-B's headquarters on Park Avenue but her phone was already jumping off its cradle. "Hello, Mr. Wirthel, how is the weather down there in Palm Beach…? Glad to hear it.… Yes, *of course* I read about her and I thought of your collection instantly. What I plan to do for you is—" she realized she was vamping wildly but knew she was good at it "—is get to the executors of the estate, find out who the beneficiaries are. Then we'll aim for an exclusive sales contract for the whole kit and caboodle.… Believe me, Mr. Wirthel, you'll absolutely be the first to hear when we know anything concrete.… Mmm-hmm, we'll try to set up a viewing for you and your charming wife as well. I will give it my utmost attention, you may be sure of it.… My best to you both."

As she was hanging up, a tall and handsome young man wearing a designer suit and a distracted expression appeared in her office doorway. He waved his newspaper and groaned, "Can you believe it?"

"Can we get in on it, is what I want to know, Dennis," Constance rejoined. "Listen, I haven't spoken with Mr. Buck yet, but I think the Vernay affair should take total precedence over anything else we're working on."

Dennis sank into an Adam-style mahogany-and-leather armchair. It was part of the smart office furniture Villiers, Buck had bestowed upon the first woman to reach the rank of vice president. "Even the Guinzberg sale?"

"Hey, if even half of the stories are true, this Vernay collection would make Guinzberg's look like a garage sale!" She grabbed a fresh pad of paper and started scribbling notes to herself. "What I want us to do is find out who's got the old lady's will and, if possible, what's in it."

"Up to your clever tricks, Constance?" The voice came from the doorway. A lean, saturnine-looking man, instantly identifiable by his tailoring and accent as British, was leaning against the doorframe. Dennis Morton respectfully rose from his seat and Constance straightened her spine. It was Ian Buck of Villiers-Same. "Will you use your legendary charm and wit to earn us a bit of business out of this Vernay affair?"

"Yes, sir."

"I have every confidence . . ." Ian Buck was gone as silently as he'd arrived.

"What did I tell you?" Constance whispered urgently to her assistant, leaning across the desk. "Full speed ahead and damn the torpedoes!"

"I'll call my contacts and see what they know about Vernay. If I hit pay dirt, will you marry me?"

"Stop trying to change the subject." She grinned. "And for the record, I do *not* date younger men."

"It's only a seven-year difference." Dennis rose dutifully. "And anyway, I'm aging rapidly. In *this* job—very rapidly." But his boss was already making her next call.

The first part of the plan was easy to execute. News of the Marquise de Vernay's death set the tightly knit, fiercely competitive Manhattan art world throbbing with excitement. Telephone lines hummed from gallery to dealer to collector to reporter and back again. By noon, this well-oiled machine had unearthed the fact that the attorneys in charge of Augustine's will and bequests were none other than Cutting, Menlow and Wilmot.

"Yahoo!" crowed Constance as her fingers—overdue for a manicure, she noticed ruefully—danced over the buttons of her phone. Once again, her natural gregariousness had turned into a professional asset. Because a fellow member of the St. Barnabas School Parents' League also just happened to be an assistant to Morgan Menlow III.

"Hi, Caroline, it's Connie Nathan. I apologize if I'm keeping you from lunch...oh, no time for lunch today? Can I guess why? Caroline, you know there are *no* secrets in this business. It's all over town that your firm is executor. And I was wondering... *What?* I can't believe it, but thanks so much. If there's ever anything I can do for you, anytime..."

Shock immobilized her for a few moments but was quickly followed by wild elation. "Doreen, this is Connie. Is Mr. Buck there? I have some very, very good news for him." Good news indeed! What her fellow St. Barnabas parent had whispered was that Villiers, Buck was mentioned by name in the will of the Marquise de Vernay. A representative of the auction house was requested to attend the reading Thursday at nine a.m. in the attorneys' offices.

"Quite a feather in your cap, my dear." Ian Buck was almost purring with delight as he thought about it. "And looking ahead to any sale which may result, I can't think of anyone more suited to be our team captain, so to speak."

"Mr. Buck, thank you so much! Believe me—" she was stammering slightly with surprise and delight "—I will give this my supreme, absolutely ultimate effort." Hanging up, she wanted to sit back and savor it for a moment. She had, in effect, just been promoted to the topmost ranks of the firm. Only the most senior, most savvy, most trusted executives were deputized by Ian Buck to direct one of the auction house's sales. Without exception, those deputies had always been male *and* aristocratic Britons or Frenchmen, to boot. Little Connie Fischer Nathan from West End Avenue had never been in their league—until now!

Now she was ensconced in antiqued, decorated-to-death splendor in a corner office on Park Avenue, looking right at an infamously expensive condominium building where the penthouse apartments had pools in them, for heaven's sake.

Now she was going to be jetting about, visiting her favorite clients, letting them know just which treasures from the Vernay Collection were so right for them that they simply must bid. Now she was going to be seeing, touching, enjoying one of the greatest art collections of modern times. "Thank you, Augustine," she muttered to the shade of the millionairess. "I don't know why you picked us, but thanks a lot, old girl."

The sight of one of those high-in-the-sky condo pools glimmering in the sunlight brought her back to earth. No matter where in the apartment they might be hiding, Jeremy's skates would not fit him. His shoe size had increased by two since last winter. Constance grabbed a dog-eared copy of the Yellow Pages from the bottom drawer of her desk. Under "Skating Equipment and Supplies" she found the number for Peck & Goodie. It took just a few minutes for them to go through their files, determine which style Jeremy liked and place the order. "Please send them here to my office, by Friday noon at the latest—or I am a mother in disgrace!"

BUT IT WAS ONLY Wednesday when she heard further Vernay news that deflated some of the high spirits at Villiers, Buck. The bulletin came through official channels; Cutting, Menlow and Wilmot mentioned in their letter about the reading that the auction house was not the only non-family party invited to hear about the late Marquise's bequests.

"Oh, God, not the New York," Dennis Morton moaned.

Connie had to agree with him. "If it had to be any museum, why did it have to be them?" she asked Augustine's ghost. The New York Museum of Art was the biggest, richest and most aggressive institution in America. Its cadres of benefactors and attorneys and curators saw to it that the New York got the cream of every crop. Only last month they had persuaded the elderly financier Nicol Guinzberg—whom Ian Buck had personally been wooing for years—to donate a sizable portion of his illustrated manuscript collection to them outright. That donation was bad for Villiers, Buck in two ways: it diminished the size and importance of the upcoming Guinzberg auction they'd been planning for so long; and it meant that those manuscripts would be forever locked behind the walls of the New York, never to be for sale again.

"What did the old girl give them—or any other museum—before this?" she wondered.

Dennis shook his sheaf of papers in perplexity. "That's the kicker—nothing."

"*Nothing?* Nada—zip—zero?" His nod of assent lifted her spirits. "Then maybe we're overreacting to this. I mean, why would she suddenly get so charitable after her death when she wasn't in life? It doesn't make sense." She waggled her crossed leg in its jade-colored French pantyhose—outrageous prices, she admitted to herself, but colors to accent an outfit that you simply couldn't get in any other brand—and stared at the tiles on the restaurant floor.

Venezia Azzuro was the latest super-hot Manhattan eatery, so fashionable it was almost impossible for ordinary mortals to book a table. But Connie's adept coddling of her wealthy clients—and her lavish expense account—made her a well-known figure to the maitre d' Tino. And she had promised Dennis a splendid lunch in return for rush research into the Marquise's history of charity. Why would a woman who never gave away a nickel, as far as anybody knew, mention a museum in her will?

She was jolted out of her trance as the waiter rolled up a brass cart. This was the famous Venezia Azzuro dessert assortment. The food critic from the *Times* had described it as "explosive in its splendor, palate-numbing in variety." Dennis's mouth had fallen open at the sight of five vertical, stacked feet of cakes, tarts, cream rolls, pastries, sauces and sweets. "Dominic," she said with a laugh, "I think Mr. Morton will have one of everything."

"And you, Signora?"

Now, what was the least caloric item on the cart? "I'll have the raspberries."

"A little zabaglione on the berries, surely?"

"I shouldn't . . ."

"Aw, c'mon Connie," Dennis urged. "You're almost too thin."

The waiter knew fading resolve when he saw it and quickly began to generously ladle the creamy, golden, oh-so-rich-and-luscious sauce on the mound of plump red berries in their crystal bowl. All three of them sighed in satisfaction.

Dennis ordered the *Piatto Dilettévole*, which, sure enough, let him have a taste of everything on the wagon. He ate almost as fast as Jeremy, Connie noted, though much more neatly. In between mouthfuls he said wistfully, "Maybe the Marquise was just bringing in the Museum to help us appraise the estate."

"We can hope. But given their style, once they've got a toe in the door, they'll start grabbing for the goodies, just the way they did with Mr. Guinzberg. No, I'm afraid we're in for one hell of a fight."

FOLLOWING THAT PHILOSOPHY, she dressed for battle on Friday morning. Her new gray-taupe cashmere suit was businesslike, yet most flattering. She also donned the big gold accessories that the saleswoman at Bergdorf Goodman had assured her "really make the look." And into her ample brown crocodile tote bag, she stuffed every bit of information on the Vernay estate that she and her staff had been able to glean.

"Are you ready, Jeremy?" she called into his room on the way to the hall coat closet. But his dishevelled book bag, sitting on the console table, gave the silent answer—no. "Young man, there will be people waiting for us in the limo!" It was a tribute to Constance's motherly skills and experience that, by the time the doorman's buzzer sounded, her son was almost completely dressed and assembled.

"How come we have a limo today, Mom?" he piped as she hustled him into the elevator with a firm hand on his shoulder.

"Because today I am going to a very, very important meeting downtown. The company is paying for it so all of us will be sure to get there on time. And the other people who'll be riding with us were kind enough to allow extra time so we could drop you off at St. Barnabas. So we must be polite and prompt for them."

"Oh." Whether the lesson in manners had penetrated or not was unclear.

A brisk January wind swept down West End Avenue and into their faces as the doorman pulled on the big bronze door. "Have a good day, Mrs. Nathan, Jeremy."

"Thank you, José. I really, really hope we do." At the curb sat a navy-blue Cadillac, which had been stretched by some customizing shop to approximately three times its original length.

"Wow!" breathed Jeremy.

"*Wow* is right" she concurred. As they approached, the driver's door popped open and a uniformed chauffeur leaped to open another one amidships. Occupying the rich interior were Dennis Morton and not one, not two, but three attorneys from Villiers, Buck. As they swept in splendor across the wintry landscape of Central Park, Jeremy explored the wonders of the limo and the adults exchanged pleasantries. Finally, Connie could restrain herself no longer. "What do you think?" she asked the legal trio.

"The word is that the New York expects to be chief beneficiary of the Vernay estate." Justin Jerrold was the senior and most serious of the three. "We suspect they have somehow learned the contents of the will." Gloom settled upon the Cadillac, only temporarily relieved by the cheery bustle of parents and children outside St. Barnabas's Georgian brick building. The rest of the ride down to Wall Street was spent in silence. Connie was rehearsing what she would tell Ian Buck if the Vernay bounty escaped them and she suspected her fellow riders were doing the same.

CUTTING, MENLOW AND WILMOT was a conservative, old-line law firm—so old-line that its offices looked unchanged from the first decades of the century. Heavy mahogany furniture, dark carpet and semisufficient lighting were the themes of the reception area. From the gloom, two white-haired women glided silently up to meet the Villiers, Buck party; they were in black taffeta dresses with white organdy collars and cuffs.

"Maids?" Connie muttered incredulously to Justin Jerrold. "In an office?"

"There used to be maids in every law office," he muttered back. "To serve tea and such. But I do believe Cutting, Menlow has the last of 'em."

The Last of Wall Street's Maids efficiently collected coats and ushered the group into a large conference room. Connie sat on a long, tufted leather couch—1920s reproduction, she noted expertly—between the lawyer and Dennis Morton. In honor of the occasion, her assistant had switched from his usual trendy suit to his most subdued attire.

The stage was set for battle all right, she observed. There were three banks of seating arranged in a square, the fourth side consisting of a gigantic leather-topped desk. This was no reproduction, but a genuine early nineteenth-century English partners' desk—so named because each side included a set of drawers, thus allowing it to serve as a joint work area for business partners. It was of golden yew, about as big as a Ping-Pong table and fitted with fine, gleaming brass handles and trim. *Hmm, I wonder what we could get for that,* Connie thought, forgetting how conditioned by her job she was.

Her attention was brought back to the business at hand by the snapping sounds of lawyers' attachés being opened. Looking around the square it was easy to figure out who the players were. To the left of the Villiers, Buck contingent sat the Family. They *had* to be the Family because several of them had the same aquiline nose and fierce expression as the late Augustine. This side of the square was clearly less than thrilled at finding they had to share the occasion with outsiders. The Family alternated between glaring to the left and right and whispering urgently among themselves.

"Didn't they know?" Connie asked Jerrold.

"Apparently the Carmodys were unaware that the will stipulated our attendance or—" the lawyer cleared his throat delicately "—that it mentioned anyone outside the family circle."

"Their spies weren't as good as our spies?"

"Exactly. And given the record of the dear departed as to charitable donations..."

"Which is *none*."

"We can hardly blame them for being, shall we say, a bit taken aback by the prospect of the Vernay estate going to the Museum."

The best she could do to conceal her chuckles was to bury her head in the big crocodile bag, feigning a search for something. This was going to be pure theater! The Family, which has waited patiently for decades to inherit the fabled Carmody wealth, now discovers it may be jilted!

And what made it even better, even more enjoyable, was that a jilted Family would undoubtedly do their legal best to pry the treasure loose from the grasp of the New York Museum of Art. Which would spell OPPORTUNITY for Villiers, Buck.

Connie looked up and directly across the room at the enemy. True to its reputation the New York had dispatched a large and efficient squad of troops for this skirmish. There were suave-looking lawyers and serious, academic types who had to be curators and conservators. There was the Museum's flamboyant director, the volatile Emilio Sant'Angelo. Next to him was a stunningly beautiful—and stunningly bejewelled—blonde whose face was becoming a fixture on the art scene. She was the third wife of a financial titan who was now courting social prominence by giving buckets and buckets of money to the New York.

Sitting beyond the elegant Mrs. Danzell, however, was a man Connie couldn't place—although she immediately wanted to. He was dressed a bit more casually than the rest of the troops. In fact, he was wearing a blazer—well-tailored, probably custom—with flannel slacks and tasselled slip-on shoes. Mr. Unidentified was also by far the best-looking man in the room—at least six-two, with that combination of dark hair and light blue eyes she'd always found riveting. He looked smart, cultivated, fun. Could it be possible? He also did *not* look married! No, there was no ring....

She elbowed Dennis discreetly. "Who's the guy in the sports jacket, beside LouLou Danzell?"

Her assistant gaped at her. "Don't you know? That's *Considine*." He used the tone of voice one would employ when referring to the Black Plague or, perhaps, Hitler.

"Ladies and gentlemen, good morning. Shall we begin?" A smooth-talking partner of Cutting, Menlow and Wilmot took a chair behind the desk. Ceremoniously, he untied the ribbons of an accordion file folder and pulled out the all important document.

2

"IF SHE MEANT TO LEAVE a battle behind her, she surely succeeded." One of the Museum's attorneys was an old friend of Justin Jerrold's; he broke ranks to come over and exchange greetings. "This one could be in litigation for years."

Everyone in the conference chamber, with the exception of the man who'd read the will aloud, wore a stunned expression by the time he had finished. It was absolutely unprecedented. It was outrageous. It was totally unworkable! The old Marquise had crafted a legacy which positively guaranteed open warfare among the parties in the room.

The document began with a bang—there was virtually no money left in the estate. "Over the course of my life," Augustine had dictated,

> I have lost faith in the value of any nation's currency. The franc, the pound, the dollar—all are at the mercy of foolish politicians and may become totally worthless. Gold and silver have their intrinsic value, but lack beauty and spirit. That is why I have selected to convert my money into objects that give me joy and remain always precious.

After that came a brief tribute to her last husband, the world-renowned art expert Marquis Thierry de Vernay whom she qualified as "the only *true* gentleman I ever met." On his deathbed, she recalled, he had begged her to let the world see the treasures they had accumulated. Now, upon her own death, she would accede to his wishes. The public would be allowed to view, perhaps even own, the Vernay Collection.

At the mention of *viewing* the forces of the New York stirred and rustled in anticipation. But the word *own* set Connie's heart to pounding. An auction, there was going to be an auction of the Vernay Collection! Across the way she saw the Family brighten considerably.

It turned out they were all wrong—and right. The will went on:

> I give and bequeath any and all portions of my estate to the New York Museum of Art, providing that the Museum can prove it does not own an identical or comparable object. Further, the Museum must agree to display each of my gifts prominently. Nothing is to be simply stored in their warehouses, as has happened with so many other bequests. Any and everything that duplicates a Museum holding must be sold to the highest bidder at public auction. The proceeds shall be divided evenly among the following people...

Then there was a list of names. Each one as it was read transformed a face on the Family side of the square from gloom to serenity.

But Augustine had not been universally benevolent. "This bequest specifically excludes my great-grand-nephew Ernest Richardson, who has no appreciation for beauty and is to get nothing." A moustached man at the end of the row deflated like a punctured balloon.

The document went on to attack the probity and professionalism of several major auction companies that had aroused the ire of the pugnacious Augustine. "I therefore direct that the sale shall be conducted by the American branch of Villiers, Buck & Company."

The man from Cutting, Menlow closed the folder and gazed serenely at his audience. "And that, ladies and gentlemen, concludes the will."

Was it good news or wasn't it? Connie looked to her fellow-workers for clues, then sneaked a quick peek at the ravishing—though apparently dangerous—man from the Museum. Considine, Dennis had said. Mr. Considine was looking baffled, too, but in a most attractive way. She tore her eyes away from him reluctantly as Dennis asked, "What do we do now?"

"Now we hear from the Family." She nodded in the direction of assorted Carmodys who were, in fact, making their way across the room. "They want to consult with their new partners—because that's what we're going to be. Partners in keeping as much of Augustine's estate as possible out of the New York's hands. And then getting the best sale prices."

Hands were shaken, cards and phone numbers exchanged. Connie was introduced by Justin Jerrold as "Our Number One sales executive." Flushed with pleasure, she turned to thank him—and locked eyes with the dazzling museum man. Mr. Considine had, it seemed, been eyeing *her*. A little thrill ran pleasurably from her head to toes, and left her throbbing.

She was still feeling the warm wave as she climbed back into the waiting limousine. *Must get back to business,* she told herself firmly. Nothing is more of a pathetic cliché than the man-hungry Manhattan divorcée lusting after anything in pants. Still, she had to wait a moment before speaking. "Well, Justin, do we sue the Museum or do they sue us?"

"No, no." The lawyer shook his head emphatically. "It is an absolute necessity that this entire affair avoid court jurisdiction. There are three compelling reasons why." Like a teacher, he ticked them off on his fingers. "First, the legal process would delay distribution of the assets, possibly for years."

Connie winced. She could practically taste the glories of a Vernay sale. To have it delayed and dragged out would be awful.

"Second, a public wrangle would lessen the cachet and value of the collection overall. And thirdly, any public discussion of monetary issues is an open invitation for the Internal Revenue Service to step in."

Connie and Dennis simply nodded in acknowledgement; the lawyer's reasoning was irrefutable. "Then what is our next step?"

"I believe we are looking at protracted negotiations aimed at a set of guidelines regulating dispersal of the Marquise's assets."

In other words, everybody's attorneys would haggle and settle it somehow. Unbidden, her mind went back to the man with the dark hair and blue eyes. If he could do that to her with just his eyes, imagine... She was feeling warm again. "So, Dennis, tell me about this Considine guy. Who is he and why's he so bad?"

Dennis stared at her. "Didn't you read...? No, I guess you didn't. It was over the holidays, when you took Jeremy down to Disney World."

"What was during the holidays?"

"Considine's interview in the *Times*. He's the new Director of Acquisitions at the New York. They hired him from the Ardsley Museum in Cleveland, right after he convinced that old couple who made a mint in office supplies—"

"The Kimmelmans," Connie prompted.

"Right, the Kimmelmans. Well, Considine apparently got them to promise to donate their entire Rodin and Brancusi holdings to the Ardsley, *plus* a check for fifteen million dollars to build a wing for display!"

"Slick operator," she observed. From only her brief exposure to Mr. Considine she could guess just how charming he might be.

"Anyway, the reporter asked what he thought of the New York art scene. And the guy said—I've got it memorized—'To the objective viewer, this is a market of rampantly inflated values and exaggerated private greed.' Who's to blame? the *Times* asked. Mr. Brand-New-From-Cleveland said the problem was caused by big, avaricious auction houses."

"Oh, great," Connie moaned.

"Right. He went on at some length about what scum we all are, how we're robbing the public of all these treasures and hawking them to nouveaux riche bandits who stole the money from the pockets of the working man. I've got the clipping pinned to my office wall. I'll make a copy for you."

Rats! she fumed silently. As if it weren't hard enough for any single woman to meet men—all the more so when you're a divorced mother—when I finally find a hot prospect he's going to hate me because of my job! And I'm probably going to hate him. She slumped glumly back into the pearl-gray leather seat. She found meager consolation in the thought that maybe there already was a Mrs. Considine. Though he didn't look married, and you usually could tell. She wanted to ask Dennis if there had been any mention of marital status in the explosive article, but didn't dare.

AFTER THE EMOTIONAL HIGH of the will-reading the following days were a marked letdown. Connie tried to concentrate on the coming Guinzberg sale; old Mr. Guinzberg was a charming raconteur and a sophisticated collector. In pre-Vernay days she would have been totally absorbed by arrangements for his auction. Those two adorable Fragonards might even set a price record if the publicity department generated the right kind of excitement.

But her mind kept straying to the legendary splendors of Augustine's hoard—the unavoidable duel with the New York...and the man who was part of it. If she'd ever been able to banish the topic from her thoughts, the fever-pitch gossip level at the office—fed by the appearance of squads of lawyers meeting day after day—would have brought it right back.

It was a little more than a month since the Vernay obituary and she was in the great sales hall of Villiers, Buck supervising the Guinzberg setup and double-checking security. Actually, Connie was down on her hands and knees, inspecting what looked like a frayed or broken wire in the alarm system.

Behind her, there was a crash, followed by a loud male curse; Dennis had run into a stack of folding chairs and barked his shin. Hopping about in pain, he squawked, "Connie, Mr. Buck wants you in his office."

This was it! No question! Unless it was a very, very major meeting, Ian Buck much preferred dropping by an employee's desk to a formal gathering in his own office. Tugging at her skirt and jacket and checking her hair in every reflective surface she passed, she made haste to the top floor suite. It was the classic English gentleman's quarters—glossily burnished fine woods, muted carpets, accents of brass and sparkling crystal.

Her boss rose as she entered, as did Justin Jerrold and the other men in the room. "Ah, here is the young lady we've been talking about," Buck said. "Constance, I'm sure you will be as delighted as I was to hear that our mutual representatives have settled on a procedure for the Vernay Collection."

She couldn't move, couldn't breathe. Frozen, she waited for his next words.

"The first step will be a complete inventory of the estate, to be conducted jointly by ourselves and the New York Museum of Art. We expect the greater part of the collection will be found in the Marquise's New York residence . . ."

"But of course we'll cover the other houses and apartments," someone interjected. He must be from the Museum, Connie thought. Nobody at the auction house would ever interrupt Ian Buck.

"Yes, surely" her boss continued smoothly. "And after the inventory each team will correlate their lists with the Museum's holdings. They will also be asked to estimate a sale price for each item." He was winding up for the punch line. "As our team representative here in Manhattan, Constance, we have selected you."

Her breath rushed out in a gasp. "Oh, Mr. B-Buck!" she stammered. "I'm so honored . . ."

"And most capable, as we all know." The rest of the crew gathered around to shake her hand, though she could tell it was practically killing some of her fellow sales executives to see this prize go to someone younger and *female*, at that.

Riding downstairs in Ian Buck's private elevator, her brain clicked forward to the next item. "Who's the team captain from the New York?" she asked Justin Jerrold.

The lawyer wrinkled his forehead. "It's somebody new. Director of Acquisitions, I heard. Constantine? Or was it Connors?"

Connie's heart started pounding again at the memory of blue eyes. "Considine," she corrected quietly. And gave the elevator's floor a great big smile.

3

"MOM. MOM! You've got to take this."

She had made the mistake of describing the coming project to Jeremy as "sort of like searching for treasure in a castle." Since then, he had been peppering her with suggested equipment for the job—the kind a seven-year-old boy would consider necessary. His Indiana Jones hat. His talking computer. A telescope. A miner's helmet with attached lamp. Each idea she had accepted with the maximum enthusiasm possible while one was assembling files.

With the full resources of Villiers, Buck's research department behind her, plus the vast, informal network of friends and informants, Constance had devoted the past week to finding out everything possible about the holdings of the New York Museum of Art. What was hanging or standing or sitting in their galleries—even the most remote, rarely visited ones? What had they disposed of as superfluous? And, most important, what was hidden in the New York's attics and cellars and storage vaults?

Old Augustine had been onto something there; it was common knowledge—at least to art professionals—that the Museum often accepted donations from a collector's estate without the space for or intention of ever displaying them. Mr. and Mrs. Gotrocks would go off to their reward with visions of The Gotrocks Gallery at the New York Museum in their heads. But when the works were delivered, curators could well assign their treasures to storage without even opening the crates.

So, as Connie Nathan said to her staff in a pep talk, "It's our job to find out what they're hiding as well as what they're showing. Let's go back over their record of donations, acquisitions and dispersals from the day the New York was founded—maybe even *before* that. What was in the MacLeod Collection? What did the Ravenels have? The Suydams?" These were the three benefactor families who had jointly created the New York as a public institution in the 1880s.

The result of her request was a stack of computer printouts several inches thick. And just last night—the night before the great Vernay adventure was to begin—Dennis had sheepishly admitted that, due to a programming error, the computer had not arranged the information as she'd asked. Instead of neat sections labeled "Paintings—seventeenth century" and "Porcelains—French," it was all just one big, messy list of furniture and manuscripts and medieval armor. After Jeremy went to bed she spent the whole evening on the kitchen floor, cutting and pasting, and then got up early to finish the job.

Now here it was *the* day and she stood in front of her closet paralyzed with indecision.

"What does one wear," she asked the orderly rows of suits and sweaters and shoes and sportswear, "on what is probably the most important day of one's entire career?" The logical answer would be her new cashmere suit. This was, of course, ignoring the fact that *he* had already seen her in it at the reading of the will. *He* might be the enemy, but that made it all the more imperative to present a smashing appearance. The usual fallback would have been the bright-yellow designer turnout; only wasn't that a bit too festive for going through a dead person's belongings? Then there was the pale green wool dress with the flattering draped neckline . . . quite suitable, but she had a sneaking suspicion that celadon green made her look a bit tired.

"Mom, Mom! You've got to take this!" Jeremy was in the doorway with a large white contraption that looked like a vacuum cleaner designed by space aliens.

"Whatever is that?"

"Dad got it for me to use at the beach." Her son described the thing's function and how it could help her search for treasure.

"Well, I'll be . . . Young man, you've just had a brilliant idea!" Constance swooped him into her arms with a big kiss. He was getting to the age, she noted sadly, where such displays of maternal affection made him edgy.

"Aw, gee." He shuffled his feet and wriggled in her embrace, flattered and nervous at the same time.

Kind of the way *I* feel about this job, she thought wryly. Reluctantly, she let the little boy go. "Better go pack your book bag, hon." Then she went back to staring at the closet.

A zippered garment bag at the far end taunted her. Should she? Would she? The bag held her very best suit, the most expensive outfit she'd ever treated herself to—a real Chanel suit. Well, it was a prêt-à-porter model, not the megabucks couture line, but you could hardly tell the difference. It was a dazzling, clear-red, nubby-soft wool which hung perfectly from the shoulders and hips. A light brass chain snaked its way through the hem of the jacket to weight it, make it hang even better. Trademark double C brass buttons shone smartly on the bodice and cuffs and the whole thing was lined in real silk imprinted with the same trademark. In short, a total dream. She'd bought it on a business trip to Paris two years before, planning to wear it as matron of honor at an old friend's third marriage.

Connie sighed in perplexity. She'd sort of classified the Chanel as For-Social-Purposes-Only—but this day simply cried out for it. There were the black sling-back pumps for accompaniment and up on the shelf was a quilted black bag with a chain handle. Might as well go for it, wear the whole Chanel shebang.

"Gee, Mom, you look pretty." Jeremy was back and—miracle of miracles—he was fully dressed with book bag slung over one shoulder.

"Well thank you, kind sir. And thank you for being ready on time." Next stop was the hall closet to extract the boy's uniform coat and her own black cashmere shell. *Grab the purse, the briefcase and the white plastic machine.* "We're gone."

EIGHT A.M. ON WEST END AVENUE meant brisk competition for cabs. She could see at least five other people up the street waving their arms at any yellow vehicle, occupied or not. But Constance had created a sign language that spoke to New York cabdrivers—and said the things they liked to hear. First, she stuck out her right hand with two fingers extended, meaning "two stops" and a good fare on the meter. Then she pointed vigorously toward the east, signifying "East Side." That was the Gold Coast of Manhattan and paradise for cabbies, where riders literally fought to get a taxi and lavish tipping was the norm.

As usual, it worked. A battered yellow Plymouth turned the corner two blocks away and was slowing down to pick up a man wearing a mink coat and homburg. Then the driver spotted Constance's semaphore; the cab accelerated rapidly, leaving the minked man grasping at air and screamed to a halt in front of mother and son.

"First stop is Ninetieth and Lex," she shouted through the cloudy bulletproof divider, wrestling with the white plastic machine.

"Where second?" the driver yelled back with a heavy accent. The ID card next to the meter, she saw, held a name with so many consonants and so few vowels that it was impossible even to guess at its pronunciation. "Sutton Circle."

"Is good," he grunted and hit the accelerator so hard his passengers were flung back against the seat. They were in front of St. Barnabas in no time.

"Gee, I hope you find a lot of treasure. You be sure to use my machine, huh, Mom? Huh?" Jeremy was trying to avoid being kissed by his mother in full view of his schoolmates.

"I sure will, J. And you learn a lot today and try to remember to bring your gym uniform home for washing, okay?" He nodded yes and plunged into the heaving sea of blue-clad boys making loud male-type noises and getting into male-type trouble. Every day she abandoned him to this boys' world she worried about Jeremy. Would he get bullied? Would he be hurt? But she knew there was virtually nothing a mother could do to shield a son. All the women she knew agreed—girls were easier to raise.

The moment the car door slammed, the driver hit the gas again. They careened wildly down the East Side, toward the East River. The streets got wider and cleaner, the buildings grander and the people on the sidewalks more elegant and self-assured.

The most self-assured little enclave in Manhattan was Sutton Circle: it took *real* money to get there. Not new money, either. As her friend Caroline from Cutting, Menlow and Wilmot had put it, "Sutton Place means you're rich. Sutton Mews means you're super-rich. But Sutton *Circle* means your grandfather was super-rich and you've held on to every penny."

Young Constance Fischer had known a girl from Sutton Circle when they were both students at Miss Whitney's Academy. If Miss Whitney's was a step up for a girl from West End Avenue, it was certainly a step down for a young lady from the East Side's toniest block. Lucia Butterworth—for that was the girl's name—was the despair of the Social Registered, Mayflower-descended Butterworth family. She'd been expelled from two of the East Coast's most exclusive boarding schools and then two more day schools in Manhattan, due to her abhorrence of studying and fondness for "having a hoot." Naturally, Connie and her classmates thought Lucia was great fun.

Lucia had even invited a gang of girls to the fabled Butterworth mansion for a "hoot" one evening. The handsome Palladian-style residence had stood gleaming-white on the corner where Sutton Circle intersected with Sutton Place. Constance Nathan could still remember her feelings of awe and admiration on entering that house. It wasn't flashy or ostentatious, but somehow you knew that everything in it was the very best, absolute perfection. She was only fifteen but remembered details clearly; it was the first time she'd ever *noticed* decor and art objects. So maybe Lucia Butterworth had, in a way, given her career guidance.

Lucia's stay at Miss Whitney's, however, lasted no longer than at any other institution of learning. There was a new mayor in office and one of his campaign pledges was a crackdown on after-hours joints—unlicensed clubs that opened up after regular bars had to close at 4:00 a.m. and served liquor, illegally, to almost anybody. The *Daily News* had a spicy photo to go with their headline Cops Bust Society Club. The aristocratic brunette seen biting an arresting policewoman on the hand was, unmistakably, Lucia Butterworth. Miss Whitney herself returned from semiretirement to expel Lucia who, four months later, ran off to Europe with a titled Spanish race-car driver.

It didn't seem that long ago, Connie thought nostalgically, but even Sutton Circle had changed a lot. Gone were the Butterworth mansion and other private dwellings around it. In their place were glossy apartment towers with wide windows and ample balconies—so much easier and less expensive to maintain. "Financial reality catches up even with the superrich," she said to herself with a laugh.

"What is number of building?" the driver asked, interrupting her reverie.

"Uh . . . fifty-eight." They looked left and right at apartment-house canopies, heading toward the river. The car was just opposite number fifty-two when she spotted it. "Oh, my God."

"Is very big house," the guttural accent concurred. "Much, much money there."

"You said it, pal." Connie was fumbling in her wallet for bills, unable to tear her gaze away from the Vernay mansion.

Like a vision out of time-travel, it had stayed unchanged as the world about it had convulsed and shrunk. A Victorian stone pile, it flaunted the turrets and balconies and mullioned windows that in 1880 were the fashionable way to let the world know just how rich you'd become. Not only that, but in a real-estate market where mere feet of ground could cost millions, the Vernay mansion had *a lawn* which extended graciously toward the East River. Around all this anachronistic splendor marched a high, strong, cast-iron fence.

Connie struggled again with the white plastic gizmo while pocketing her change. The driver muttered something she interpreted as "Have a nice day," then he made a high-velocity U-Turn and sped off like lightning toward Sutton Place.

Before she could reach the massive gate, a guard with a huge German shepherd beside him was there to challenge her. The actual words were "May I help you?" but it was clear that persons with no business at the Vernay Mansion would never gain entry. Good—Cutting, Menlow and Wilmot said they had hired the best security firm in the business to safeguard the estate.

"I'm Constance Nathan from Villiers, Buck."

"May I see two pieces of identification, please." It was not a question. The guard had the close-cropped hair and ramrod posture of a Marine. His eyes gazed at her firmly from his bronze face.

The white machine clipped her ankle painfully as she put it down to open her purse. While driver's license and employee ID were being studied intently, she found her eyes drawn back to the stone hulk behind the fence. Slate-capped turrets finished off each sprawling wing and the one nearest the river was the largest. *What a view there must be from those windows!* She whistled quietly. Although some were overgrown with ivy, which swarmed over the entire face of the building, the windows that could be seen appeared to be blocked; probably the executors had pulled the draperies or shutters when they sealed the house. A light crust of snow lay on the ground, soiled only by the guard's footprints leading to and from the entrance portico....

Damn! She had intentionally dropped Jeremy off at school ahead of the usual time, so she would be here before 9:00 a.m.—and one up on the aggressive Mr. Considine.

But there he was, nonchalantly leaning against a pillar on the portico, his trench coat jauntily askew so the Burberry lining showed. Constance gritted her teeth.

The guard passed her identification back through the gate and unlocked it. He pointed at the clunky apparatus she was toting. "May I help you with that, Mrs. Nathan?"

"Why, yes. Thank you very much. What's *your* name?"

"Fitch, ma'am. Alfred Fitch." He managed to pick the thing up neatly without losing either the dog or his perfect posture.

"You were a Marine—am I right, Fitch?"

"Absolutely!" His teeth gleamed in a wide, warm grin. Chatting with Fitch kept her from staring at Mr. Considine as she really wanted to do. But from the corner of her eye she could see that he was just as good-looking as she remembered and that he straightened up as they approached.

"Constance Nathan?" he called out. The voice was alluring, too—somewhere between baritone and bass with an inflection that came from a gentler place than New York City.

"That's me. You must be Kenneth Considine." She trod gingerly on the ice-covered step to shake his hand. "A pleasure to meet you and I look forward to working with you." Well, at least half of that statement was true.

Under the portico's roof her eyes adjusted from the glaring reflection of sun on snow. By his feet she could see an oblong, cloth-covered case and, wrapped securely with twine, a huge, hard-covered catalogue of the sort museums use to list their possessions. *Ha!* He was making a statement already—coming to claim booty for the New York. "What's that?" she pointed sharply, although she knew.

"That?" He kicked the catalogue casually—still wearing loafers, she noticed. "We've got to have a book for recording everything and the Museum's got thousands of these things lying around. I've also got a printout of our complete inventory and—" his foot nudged the big case "—a camera and lights so we can get good photos."

"Oh." It sounded reasonable enough. Sensible.

"And may I ask what that is?" He was pointing at the white gizmo that Fitch had placed on the steps. Subconsciously she noted—*he's left-handed; no rings.*

"Uh . . . well, that's a metal detector. It's possible an eccentric like the Marquise had a safe or strongbox hidden in the walls where we might miss it. A metal detector should pick it up."

Kenneth Considine smiled at her warmly and those deadly blue eyes sparkled. "What a good idea!" he said, and she started to get that swooning feeling again.

"Actually..." Should she let him know she was an ex-married woman, a Mommy? *The hell with it.* "Actually, it was my son's idea. He's seven. My ex-husband bought it for him to scavenge loose change at the beach and he thought it would help in our, quote, 'search for buried treasure.'"

The man was still smiling. *Hallelujah!* And his face hadn't undergone that subtle shift she'd seen so many times before as a single man decided she was not eligible for his precious attentions. "Smart boy," was all he said.

"Before we begin..." Fitch interjected politely, "I would like to sketch out for you the security precautions that have been approved by Cutting, Menlow and Wilmot." He described the network of electronic, human and canine surveillance, which protected the Vernay mansion around the clock. The front door was the only one ever to be unlocked by the guard or another supervisor when both the museum and auction house representatives had arrived. Two men would be at the door all day, with a third available for delivery of supplies, food or for any other errands the team might require. The door would be locked again at 5:00 p.m. sharp, at which time the burglar-alarm system would be reactivated. Due to the great confidence all parties had in the probity of the two appraisers, they would not be searched as they left, but "We would greatly appreciate it if you would inform us of anything you remove from the house."

"Sounds sensible and prudent," Kenneth commented. It sounded all right to Constance as well; she was accustomed to having her briefcase and purse checked whenever she was in the vault at Villiers, Buck. And she was beginning to get a fix on Considine's accent; it was slightly Southern but crisp, not a drawn-out drawl.

"If you would just sign in, please." Fitch held out a logbook; she wrote "Constance F. Nathan" under "Kenneth R. Considine." *Robert?* she wondered.

"The adventure begins." He looked as excited as she felt. They picked up their paraphernalia and edged toward the huge wooden door.

Like the rest of the mansion, the portal was Gothic in a massive, Victorian way. Giant planks of wood were held together by straps of thick iron and the door knocker looked heavy enough to require two hands to lift it. In the door's center was a circular, mullioned window of amber glass, protected by a cross-hatching of yet more iron. *I'd like to see your typical New York burglar try to smash* that *in,* Connie thought ironically.

Fitch ceremoniously extracted a sealed envelope from his case and tore it open. Inside were the keys to the three locks, set securely in a metal plate. The two more modern ones opened easily enough, but the guard had to struggle with the original. He jiggled and jimmied until, with a shriek and squeal, the old-fashioned key turned.

Constance took a deep breath in anticipation and glanced at her teammate, who rolled his eyes in a comic mimicry of suspense. She laughed. Fitch pushed the door open and she craned her neck to peer into the gloom beyond.

"Oh, my God!" she exclaimed for the second time that day.

Considine was looking over her shoulder now. "Good God A'mighty!" Even in shock she registered—I was right, Southern.

Now it was Fitch's turn. Heeling his dog, he turned to look inside the Vernay mansion. His eyebrows shot up and his jaw dropped. All that came out was "Shee—"

4

THE FRONT HALL of the Vernay mansion was, of course, enormous. Later, when astonishment faded, Connie calculated that her entire apartment would fit inside it with room to spare. But what rendered her—and Kenneth Considine and Fitch—speechless was not the dimensions of the antechamber but that it was *full of things.* Absolutely chockablock, stuffed to the corners, piled to the rafters. And even the most cursory glance told them that those 'things' were Augustine Carmody Cheney d'Urso de Vernay's legacy of treasure.

There were small tables made completely of precious malachite and bronze standing on top of a gilded settee inlaid with ivory—Napoleonic Empire, probably—while on the tables perched a cluster of golden candelabra. An entire dining-room suite of Regency rosewood was stacked vertically, with the vast sideboard serving as base. A row of ornate picture frames marched out from another corner, the kind of frames that hold important paintings, while unframed canvasses were rolled and stacked like cordwood around them. The marble bust of a noble Roman peered rather wistfully from behind several Venetian glass chandeliers.

This mass of precious objects was so dense that, spacious though the hall was, now there was only a passageway wide enough for a single person to walk through. It was hard to even figure out where the walls might be; the only visible portion was hung with a splendid tapestry showing gallant courtiers and elegant ladies at a stag hunt. They were costumed in Louis XIV style.

"Real Aubusson," Connie breathed.

"It's *all* real," Kenneth said behind her.

"And it's all dirty," Fitch put in disapprovingly.

He was quite right. It had obviously been years since anyone had applied a rag or duster to any of these jumbled, splendid surfaces. The Cutting, Menlow lawyers who knew her had regaled everybody with stories of the Marquise's cantankerous miserliness. Her idea of wage scales for household staff had been cemented in the Depression, when a few dollars per week was the going rate. And the demands she'd made on "help" were monumental—no days off or limited duties here!

This had the predictable result: nobody would work for her. That nobody had in recent years was obvious from the eddies of dust, the layers of grit and the cobwebs that coated her jumbled acquisitions. "Do you suppose the rest of the house is as dirty as this?" Connie asked despairingly. She was thinking about her beautiful Chanel suit and what was going to happen to it.

"Probably," Considine agreed glumly. "What worries me is—"

"Is the whole joint jam-packed like this?" She completed his thought. "If it is, we are gonna be here for a long, long time." Suddenly, the great adventure had lost much of its luster.

In comic imitation of the courtiers in the tapestry, Kenneth bowed and swept an arm toward the interior. "Shall we check it out?"

I should have worn jeans, she thought ruefully. *And why doesn't he go first and get dirty?* But it wouldn't do to have the New York Museum of Art hear that Villiers, Buck's representative was too squeamish to get the job done. "Right," she said, and stepped forward resolutely, groping for a light switch in the gloom, praying no cobwebs would hit her in the face.

There was the switch—the old push-button kind. Light of sorts filtered down from a massive chandelier; half of its bulbs had expired, and those still functioning could be no stronger than forty watts. But at least the visitors could now see to snake their way through the maze.

Beyond the antechamber was a central hall with flagstone flooring, a granite fireplace twice as tall as Connie and a broad, majestic staircase on which a lady could make a grand entrance. Except that every step of it was almost completely covered with more of Augustine's trove. Books and folios, Chinese porcelains and carved ivory, silver chests and ornate caskets—they were lined up into the gloom of the second-floor landing. "Did you guys have any idea there was this much of it?" Connie asked.

Considine shook his head, baffled. "Absolutely not. If we had, I'd have insisted on a task force to handle it, not just the two of us. This is—" he shrugged his shoulders, searching for the word "—insanity. Who could have imagined it?"

He seemed honest, sincere, as staggered as she was. She found herself warming to Kenneth Considine, dangerous as that could be professionally. He was certainly the most attractive man she'd come across in a long time. Fit, too; she could see that from his strong shoulders, flat stomach and muscled thighs. Yes indeed, he looked good *all* over. Except—the Mommy side of her talking now—he was a little overdue for a haircut.

Back to business. "I guess we'd better check the whole house, for the record." He agreed, and they wound their slow and dusty way through the salon... library... dining room... pantry... kitchen. It was all the same story. A vast rabbit warren crammed with wonderful things and terrible dirt. Even one of the huge zinc kitchen sinks was home to a large set of gold-rimmed Meissen tableware with baronial crests.

But the kicker, the capper to the whole thing, lay in wait above. The team retraced its path back to the grand stairway and picked its way delicately up, fearful of starting an art avalanche. The main bedroom suite provided welcome relief; Augustine's chamber was actually clear enough for them to walk about normally, although treasure was perched here and there—

including on the bed. And most of the furnishings *matched*, being in the Elizabethan style.

The guest bedrooms, however, were another story. Now Constance saw that what she'd thought were shutters blocking the windows was just the mountain of furniture and bric-a-brac that filled every room. Eyeing a stack of Sheraton chairs that teetered up the ceiling, she said dryly, "I guess la Marquise didn't entertain much."

"Jesus, look at this!" Considine had gone on ahead of her into the adjoining bath. She eased her way past the chairs and poked her head through the door. Yes, the bathroom was full, like everywhere else. But what he was pointing at, his jaw slack with amazement, was the most bizarre of all.

The builders of the Vernay home had obviously been Continental in taste. Each bathroom was equipped with a European-style hand-held shower attached to the tub—and a bidet. Nestled in *this* bidet was the figure of a swan, about four feet high and three feet across. The body of the swan was composed of thousands of pure crystal beads strung on wire. Its feet, bill and eyes appeared to be of gold. Sitting on its unusual nest, it wore an expression of exceeding smugness.

Connie couldn't help it. She began to laugh in a most unprofessional and adolescent manner. Through tears of hilarity she was glad to see Considine whooping, too. Soon they were doubled over, hanging on to each other to keep from banging into anything else. Her hands were on his broad shoulders and his were clasped around her waist; that was the nicest part of all.

Abruptly, they surfaced from the pool of laughter and were looking right into each other's eyes. Self-consciously, Connie straightened up and dropped her hands. Uh-oh, she thought, I have just been very, very silly. But it was all right—he was still smiling.

"I'm glad to find out you think it's funny, too," was all he said. But it was more than that. Now they were friends, allies against this mountain of mammon built by one rich, stingy and crazy old lady.

"Call me Connie." She held out her hand and he shook it firmly, warmly. This was their real meeting, not the one on the portico.

"And I'm Ken."

SHE WAS RECALLING that handshake and the way it brought back the sensual thrill she'd had upon first seeing him as she dialed Ian Buck's home phone number that evening. Reporting to her boss should have been the very first thing on her agenda. But before that it was absolutely necessary to take a long shower and wrap the poor Chanel suit up for the dry cleaners. Then she had to feed Jeremy, read him a bedtime story and tuck him in.

Now she was ready to collapse with exhaustion, but duty called. "Mr. Buck, it's Constance. My apologies for calling so late, but the Vernay mansion is the most amazing thing I've ever seen. Her collection must be at least ten times as large as we guessed—Yes, ten times.

There isn't an empty inch in the whole house, it's all just piled up to the rafters... No, there's no common element or unifying theme. There's something there for everybody. It will make simply the most smashing auction—a week's worth, at least—*after* it's all cleaned.... Mmm-hmm, quite filthy. Do you suppose we could get a reliable, bonded cleaning service to... I see your point. Terrible security problems, and it would require changing the legal agreement. Well then, we'll just have to clean as we go.... Oh, he's Okay." She feigned a careless attitude about her teammate. "He seems much more reasonable than he sounded in that interview." Firm resolve deepened her voice. "Don't worry, Mr. Buck, nobody from the New York is going to put anything over on *me*.... How long? At this point, I'd have to say it'll take us several months to finish the job.... Certainly, I'll brief you again tomorrow. Good—" She was going to add "night" but her employer had, as always, hung up too fast.

NEXT MORNING'S RENDEZVOUS was quite a change from the first.

While Fitch was still spit-and polish perfection, the team of art experts was dressed for combat. In Connie's case that meant a set of green sweats, running shoes and a canvas knapsack to protect her notebooks. Ken had chosen well-worn Levis, heavily tooled cowboy boots and a yellow ski parka with old lift tickets dangling from the zipper. He was carrying a small vacuum cleaner and she was amused to read the notice stamped on it: Property of The New York Museum of Art. Do Not Remove.

"Well, Fitch, we may not be stylish today, but we are sensible."

"Indeed, ma'am."

"Here's a list of some supplies we need, for starters." In the cab on the way downtown, Connie had remembered that one guard was there to run errands. Might as well take advantage of it. "Three large jugs of detergent, scrub bucket, pack of sponges, five packs of paper towels. Make that jumbo packs. Fifty bucks should cover it."

"No, Mrs. Nathan." Fitch pushed the bills back into her hand. "We have an expense account and Cutting, Menlow and Wilmot will reimburse us." An expense account? These sure must be fancy security guards. She and her teammate watched as Fitch reenacted yesterday's struggle with the door locks. Once again, the almost impenetrable mass of treasure and dirt confronted them.

"Where do you want to start?" Ken's voice was glum.

"I dunno—wherever's easiest. How about the bedroom?"

"Sounds good to me." He shouldered his camera bag and catalogues and was gallantly picking up her metal detector when Connie stopped him. It clipped her ankle painfully with each step as they snaked their way through the hall and up the stairs.

Augustine's bedroom was in the big turret facing the river and its giant, palanquin-style bed was placed to take advantage of the view through curved windows. They dumped their equipment in a clear space at the bed's foot. Ken blew air through his teeth and looked around in exasperation. She nodded in agreement. "And this is as good as it gets!"

True, there was room to walk past the huge wardrobe, around the bed to the ornate chest and bedside stand. But flotsam and jetsam of the Marquise's collecting madness had washed up here as well. One side of her bed was occupied by stacks of dusty tooled-leather folios. Intrigued, Connie untied the silk bow holding the topmost. And was immediately swept into a lost world of perfection and serenity. "What is it?" Ken asked.

"What's what?"

"What you were gasping at."

She didn't even know she'd made a noise. "Japanese ukiyo-e prints, eighteenth century. By the Master Haronobu, I would say."

Ken leaned over her shoulder and she got a whiff of fresh masculine scent. After a minute's viewing, he breathed, "Perfection."

That's pretty much what I could say about you, Connie thought wryly. Up close, you could see the thickness of his lashes and pick out the one or two tiny silver hairs mixed with black on his temple. "This will really fill out our Japanese Gallery."

"What?" she yelled, diving for the notebook in her satchel. "I distinctly remember that the Ellimans donated a complete set of ukiyo-e to the Museum back in the sixties. If you don't have them on display, that's *your* problem . . ."

"Connie, Connie," he groaned comically, rolling his eyes back up into his head in exaggerated despair. "It's that damned interview I had in the *Times*, isn't it?"

Her head was in the notebook, her hands flipping pages furiously. "You mean to say you don't feel that way about private collections and auction houses? That you were misquoted or—what is it politicians always say—'taken out of context?' "

"I do feel that way and I said what I said. I believe fine art is so important to our human community that everybody should have access to it, not just the rich. But if we're going to have a fight about every single object in this house . . ."

"Here it is." She thrust the page under his nose. "1967. Bequest in memory of Benjamin Elliman—forty-seven ukiyo-e prints, provenance, a noble family from Hokkaido."

He seemed nonplussed. "Huh. I wonder where the hell they are? If it was up to me they would certainly be on display."

Connie kept on reading. "The Elliman bequest has never been publicly mounted, apparently due to lack of funds for renovation of the exhibition area."

"Huh," Ken said again. "I'll have to look into it. Meanwhile, truce?"

Who could resist a smile like that? "Truce." She picked up the portfolio again and indicated his ready camera. "Shall we? Where do you want to shoot it?"

"That looks good." He was pointing to the top of a massive coffer which, like the bed, was heavily carved and blackened with age. They cleared it and vacuumed away the worst of the dirt, though the cleaner's plug sparked nastily in the ancient electric socket.

While she was settling the portfolio in place, Connie looked up and got a surprise. "Gee, that's the only thing I've seen in this house that isn't first-rate." Above the chest hung a large oil painting of a boy in the Buster Brown hairdo and short-pants suit of the 1920s. His expression was saccharin-angelic—an expression that she knew little boys only assume when they are trying to get away with something. The whole thing, in fact, was painted in a rather maudlin style. "I guess the old girl made an occasional mistake."

"Maybe it's a family portrait." Ken was peering through the camera's viewfinder. "Could you prop that up a bit, please? And we need a number for catalogue reference."

With an index card and felt-tip pen, she established that the Haronobu print folio they'd fought over was Item Number One of the entire Vernay Collection.

5

WORD HAD GONE OUT to all interested parties—including the *very* interested Carmody family—that the Vernay residence in New York was so packed with treasure that the Nathan—Considine team was going to need several months to itemize and assess it. It was with mixed feelings that Connie and Ken heard reports from the teams that had been dispatched to Augustine's homes in Paris, Geneva and Florence. Had she piled them full of treasure, too?

The answer was negative. Each residence was formally decorated and had been empty for decades. The only similarity with the Sutton Circle house was that the European homes had also not been cleaned in what seemed like aeons. The Villiers, Buck man who had checked out the apartment with panoramic views of Lake Geneva said sympathetically to Connie, "Too bad you can't use a cleaning service." She could only agree.

The days soon settled into a routine, albeit a fascinating and challenging one. Connie was sure the other parents at St. Barnabas thought she was out of work. How else to account for the fact that when she delivered Jeremy to school she no longer wore business suits or carried an attaché case? Why else would she be wearing raggedy jeans and old running shoes? Or carrying shopping bags from her local delicatessen?

That last item had become a regular thing for reasons anyone who lived or worked around Sutton Place knew well; the neighborhood was so fancy and the rents so high that there were no food stores to be found. Nothing in the mansion's kitchen worked. If anyone wanted a simple cup of coffee—a reasonable request, given that it was cold inside as well as outside—Fitch would have to send one of his deputies on a long journey. Ramon Acevedo and Bob Lincoln didn't seem to mind but Connie felt guilty about it anyway. So at least twice a week she brought lunch makings from the famous store on Broadway—succulent Nova Scotia lox and cream cheese on bagels, shrimp salad crunchy with fresh dill, rare roast beef with horseradish dressing on old-style rye bread laced with caraway seeds.

To herself, she admitted these gestures weren't just for the benefit of the security guards. Her mother had always said the way to a man's heart is through his stomach. Connie figured it was sure worth a try with Kenneth Considine.

So far, the only fault she could find with the man was that he seldom spoke about personal things or his past and seemed to have no idea just how good-looking and sexy he was. His status as a single man had been verified not by any admissions on his part, but through her extensive network of buddies. A girlfriend who lived on Long Island had a brother who was married to a woman who came from Cleveland, who knew the story about the ambitious young curator of that city's Ardsley Museum.

It seemed that, about the time Kenneth Considine was laying successful siege to the wealthy Kimmelmans, an equally ambitious young Shaker Heights post-deb had laid successful siege to *him*! He had come to the Ardsley from a museum in Louisville, Kentucky a few years before—and driven all the sweet young things crazy with his looks and charm. But he had eluded all attempts at capture until Miss Shaker Heights decided to hunt him on his own ground. She took several crash courses in art and volunteered her services to the museum.

The story of how Kenneth Considine had wooed the millionaires into making a magnificent, munificent donation to the Ardsley was all over the Cleveland papers and there was even a lavish dinner in honor of the occasion. But when he was seen shopping in Tiffany's for a ring, the tale was all over town in a flash. In her engagement picture, Miss Shaker Heights wore an extremely pleased expression.

Things did not proceed as expected, however. The prospective bridegroom went on a business trip for a few days. When he returned to Cleveland, his fiancée got on a plane to Mustique. Alone. She did not return to the shores of Lake Erie until Kenneth Considine had moved to Manhattan.

Eventually, friends got the story out of her. *He* had simply accepted a position at the New York without saying a word to her. *He* had thus made it clear that the job was, and always would be, more important to him than she—or, by implication, any woman—could be. When confronted with his misdeed he had simply admitted that, yes, a position at the nation's most influential museum *was* his chief goal in life. He was sorry and wanted her to keep the ring, but that's the way he was.

Aha, thought Connie as she heard the story. Fair warning, my girl. You are dealing with a tough customer here.

But that was hard to believe when she saw his welcoming grin every weekday morning. Or shared his enthusiasm for another treasure they had discovered. Or found that he was perfectly willing to share the nasty cleaning chores that were the downside of their adventure.

Despite the fact that her expertise in art was less broad than his, Ken never treated her with condescension. And there was no sign of the hostility she'd expected following their skirmish about the ukiyo-e prints. Whenever they came upon something he prized for the museum, he waged a vigorous but fair fight for it. Connie would dive into the Villiers, Buck printouts while he consulted the New York's master list. If either showed duplication, he usually conceded graciously, and the thing was headed for the auction block.

But there was a flip side too—and it made Connie very, very nervous if she brooded about it before going to sleep. The atmosphere of trust and cooperation between them had to be mutual. If Ken believed there was an error in her "book" she had to give him the benefit of the doubt. A group of Tang Dynasty bronzes and four precious Russian icons were headed for the Museum's halls because her partner had explained to her at length how they differed from objects already residing there.

"What would Mr. Buck say?" she moaned to herself on her pillow and thumped it into a new shape. The chairman of Villiers, Buck was not known to forgive mistakes on the part of his staff. A mistake was anything which reduced profits for the company and anybody who committed mistakes was summarily terminated. What if Ian Buck knew that his ace dealmaker had agreed, all dewy-eyed, to give up those gorgeous Tangs, which collectors the world over would gladly pay for with their last penny? Or the icons, which were beyond price because the Russian government forbade export of them on pain of death?

The answer to these questions was obvious. So, in her nightly reports to her boss, Connie would often embroider stories about the battles she had waged on his behalf—when actually, Ken had simply said, "Okay, Connie, you're right." That way Mr. Buck would not think she was going soft, not getting the best possible deal for the auctioneers. Because reality was so very different from everybody's expectations.

"Nobody can understand who isn't in our shoes," Ken agreed. He waved a hand; in a matter of weeks they had progressed from Augustine's suite and were toiling through the third bedroom. "This is a separate world.

Leaving here at night is like...like surfacing from a deep scuba dive."

"I know." She had seen the look on his face at 5:00 p.m. as they heard the muffled peal of the front door chimes. That was Fitch's signal that the workday was over and it was time to go home. Ken always looked surprised that the hour was so late and didn't seem to want to leave. Connie was sure the same look was on her own face, but for a different reason. She did not mind abandoning the Vernay booty all that much—and was always dying for a shower—but she very much minded leaving Kenneth Considine for the night.

On a Friday when it seemed that at last winter was relaxing its grip and spring might actually come, her heart raced ahead of her intellect to the natural conclusion. The breeze that blew up the lawn from the East River had a softer edge to it, a hint of vernal fragrance. For the first time since they'd begun their work, she didn't have to rush to get gloves on. Ken had left his ski parka unzipped. The two of them signed out and wished Fitch, Ramon and Bob a good weekend.

Strolling toward the corner of Sutton Place, where they could hail cabs, Connie looked up to see Ken's face highlighted by the streetlamp above. For about the millionth time she wondered what it would be like to kiss those sensual lips, explore that great body in detail and make mad love with him. But then she felt a catch in her throat and her brain printed up the message in big type: *I am in love with this man. God help me.*

"Looks like taxis are in short supply. You want to share?" His voice jolted her out of the trance.

"Uh, sure." Ken had only been in New York a few months and it showed in his cab-summoning technique. He simply stood on the curb and raised an arm, waiting patiently for one of the precious vehicles to respond. She had to smile. "That's not going to work, Ken. This is rush hour in Manhattan."

"I don't seem to have much luck with taxis. What do you suggest?"

"More competitive methods." Connie stepped right out into the stream of traffic and went into her sign language dance for "two stops, uptown," cleverly not mentioning that the second stop was on the West Side. As usual, it worked.

"Ah, that's what separates the New York native from us arrivistes," he said with a laugh and opened the door for her. Her head was swimming as the cab crept up Madison Avenue to his apartment house. She knew she had responded to Ken's conversation but had absolutely no idea what she'd said. Through the haze she realized he gave the driver money to cover her fare as well, but she was too dazed to protest.

"See you Monday, Connie. And say hello to Jeremy for me."

"Sure. Thanks. Have a terrific weekend." A red light stopped the cab at the next corner and she turned for a last glimpse of him. As Ken greeted the doorman, another tenant was exiting—a blond woman about her own age. The woman eyed him with open admiration and speculation, lingering a bit. *I understand completely, honey,* thought Connie. And I wonder if either of us will have any luck. Maybe Ken was one of those guys who only go for blondes. Should have asked what Miss Shaker Heights looked like. If golden hair was his taste, she was doomed. Brunette she'd been born, and brunette she stayed. Friends who fought nature and went for the golden look spent more time at it than she had to spare.

Likewise, if Mr. Considine liked 'em small and cuddly, she was out of the running. She'd hit five foot eight at age twelve, and her hectic life-style kept her permanently rangy. Well, at least she was big and strong enough to do her part shovelling through old Augustine's mess.

Constance was so preoccupied with her love thunderclap that Jeremy noticed at dinner. "Mom. Mom, what's the matter?" he asked, holding a smothered pork chop in both hands.

"Oh, nothing, J. Please use your knife and fork, get your elbows off the table and don't talk with your mouth full. And wipe your hands!" The price of table manners, it seemed, was eternal vigilance. "How are things at school?"

"Okay. Hey, want to know something really terrific that happened? In gym class today—we're taking baseball this quarter—and Jessica Wilmerding stole second base. And Brian Herman—he was playing second base—he said Jessica stole it wrong and he pushed her and she hit him back and guess what?"

"What?"

"Jessica hit him and knocked out his front teeth, both of them. It was *great*!"

His mother was so taken-aback that she forgot to tell Jeremy to chew before he spoke. Here she had been worrying about what boys might do to him, when girls today engaged in fisticuffs, as well. What had happened to the time when little girls had gym class off by themselves and wore cute, tailored gym tunics and did stuff like modern dance and field hockey? "Fist fights are not 'great,' Jeremy." It was time for parental sternness. "How do you think Brian's Mommy and Daddy feel about a son who has no front teeth?"

"Well, gee, won't his big teeth be coming in pretty soon?"

Checkmate! At the last appointment Jeremy's dentist had warned that the boy's baby teeth were getting ready to make way for the permanent set. Better change the subject. "And how were things at Mrs. Wickes's?"

"Oh, okay." He casually dismissed the woman Connie thanked her lucky stars for—regularly. Mrs. Wickes was a roly-poly widow who lived on the second floor of their building and gladly cared for Jeremy and four other kids every day after school, until their working mothers got home. She was remarkable for her calm behavior as well as the pittance she charged for this service, which helped her stay in the apartment where she'd raised her own family.

"Hey, Mom, can we buy *Dragonor of the Black Planet*? Danny O'Rourke says it's *great*!"

"What is it?" Absentmindedly she heard his recital of the wonders of this cartoon series and responded that they would rent the videotape, not buy it. But her mind was sliding back to its new center of gravity—Kenneth Considine.

6

"HOW CAN YOU BE SO STUPID?" Connie growled at her image in the smudged Venetian mirror as she cleaned it. "Can't you even *talk* to him?" Now she realized that it was more than just sexual attraction she felt for Ken, she'd become almost tongue-tied in his presence. It wasn't as if there weren't plenty of available topics, but she was inhibited by fear. Fear of being obvious, fear of making a fool of herself over a man who was indifferent. And the nagging fear of the day inevitably coming when they would have to be enemies.

That would be the day their work here in the mansion was concluded. When the managements of the Museum and auction house would scrutinize and review the way she and Ken had split up the estate. Would Ian Buck decide she had given the New York a sweetheart deal and cut his own profit? Would the Museum second-guess Ken's judgment and attack hers? The two of them were like Roman gladiators; when the arena's gate opened the battle must begin.

"Whew!" Ken whistled behind her and she almost lost her footing, braced between an ancient stepladder and the mantel over which the mirror hung. He reached to steady her. "Gee, I'm sorry, Connie. I thought you saw me coming. Are you Okay?"

"Yeah, sure. Just startled. What were you whistling at?"

"That mirror—a real beauty. The beveling looks like eighteenth-century work but it's in fantastic condition."

"Mmm-hmm." When Constance had tried to catch herself, her hand had landed on a small picture frame which lay face down on the mantel. It was classic Victoriana—dark, varnished wood carved to a fare-thee-well, with dollops of gold leaf laid on with a lavish hand—not of any artistic interest or commercial value. But the picture within the frame held her attention. The young girl in it was just on the verge of womanhood, with graceful posture and long, dark hair flowing over her shoulders. She was dressed all in white—buttoned kid shoes included—and wore an expression of vulnerability, mixed with anticipation of the life ahead. The face reminded Connie of . . .

"Good grief!" She thrust the photo at Ken. "I think that's Augustine as a girl. One of the Carmodys at the will reading looked just like this."

He stared at the picture intently. "Yes, I remember. The branch of the family that came in from California."

"How do you suppose this," she asked, tapping the glass covering the photo, "turned into the Augustine we know and love? The crazy lady who cared more about things than people and lived in this . . . this rabbit warren?"

"I've been wondering about that myself." Ken raised his arms to lift her down from her perch and she was amazed at how easily and effortlessly he could lift one hundred and thirty-seven pounds. "Because I've never seen any collection remotely like this. I don't mean the size of it—plenty of collectors get obsessed, and she had more money and time than most. But what puzzles me is that there's no *theme*."

"You mean a particular era, or artist, or art form?"

"Yes, some unifying element. Every major art buyer I've heard of had something in their head that guided them in a certain direction. Like the Kimmelmans. You know who they are?"

"Of course," she responded drily. Better not let him know how much research she'd done on his life. "The office-supply millionaires. Didn't you get a donation out of them?"

"Right." He nodded matter-of-factly. "Now, when I visited their house for the first time I was a little confused. They had paintings and sculpture ranging from the Renaissance through modern times. I didn't want to ask them outright why they had such a mix."

Connie squinted at him. "Because you wanted to understand them, get inside their heads?"

"Exactly." Ken grinned gloriously at her shrewd intuitiveness. "That's how you can persuade them to give stuff away. So I went back there several times and finally got it."

"The theme?"

"Yup. The unifying element was romantic love. Every object either depicted it directly or had something romantic in its history."

"That's kind of sweet, isn't it? I mean, they didn't start collecting until they were in their sixties." *Whoops!* She was letting her research on Considine show. "At least, I remember hearing something like that," was added lamely.

"Correct. And I hadn't thought about it, but it is kind of cute."

Cute, huh? That was his opinion of a man and woman in their eighties who still loved each other enough to spend millions of dollars on art that celebrated romance? *Face it, kid,* she lectured herself, *this is a lost cause.* She waved the framed photo at the lost cause. "I think I'll have the staff back at the office do a little digging on Augustine's life. Personally, I'd like to understand what made her so weird. And if we can establish anything that'll make her a bit sympathetic to the public, I'll bet they'll be even more interested in her collection."

"Good thinking." He was rummaging through the mess on the mantel. "Look, Con, here's another piece of Fitzhugh orange." The platter was of porcelain so fine that light shone through it. And the patterns and pictures painted on it in China more than two centuries ago glowed in a fresh, shimmering apricot. "How many does that make?"

"Fitzhugh . . . Fitzhugh." She flipped through their "small" catalogue, the non-illustrated version, which

Ken had worked up on his personal computer. "Two hundred and eleven. And we're still a long way from the pantry. There's piles of it down there, remember?"

Yes, she thought resolutely, *better put away any dreams about love in* this *house and get back to work.* It was after her nightly report to Ian Buck that she remembered to phone Dennis Morton. She asked him to work up a biography of the late heiress who'd had such an impact on her own life. And heart.

THREE NIGHTS LATER she picked up his message on her home answering machine. It had become a communications center for the Vernay project by circumstance; the phone lines in the mansion itself were, like everything else there, completely worn-out. But, for security reasons, no one dared admit a repairman. The nearest street phone was two blocks away from the house and Connie was locked inside during the hours her secretary was on duty. So she'd plugged a fresh microcassette into the answering machine that sat on her kitchen counter and spent evenings catching up on communications.

"Hi, Connie. It's Dennis. I got all the dirt on *la belle Augustine* and it's pretty fascinating. Some pictures, too. I'll drop by tonight around six and leave it with the doorman if you're not free. See ya!"

"Very clever, Dennis," she muttered at the machine. "Six o'clock just happens to be dinnertime." And how could she turn away a hungry young assistant who had obviously worked overtime to get her the information she wanted? Sighing, she pulled another package of shell steaks out of the freezer and popped them into the microwave. Hitting the defrost button, she heard the fridge door whoosh open behind her.

"Hey, young man, you know the rules. No soda before dinner!" Jeremy was clutching a two-liter bottle of cola and wearing an expression of exaggerated innocence. "Juice, but no soda."

"Oh, I forgot." His acting was improving.

"Dinner in fifteen minutes, love. Will the film be finished?"

"No, but that's okay. I can watch the rest after." He went back to his room clutching a glass of orange juice as his mother marveled at how easily the kid had mastered the VCR that was hooked up to his own little TV set! Back when television in color was considered a wonder, who'd have dreamed that little boys would be able to rent a Disney film and view it at their leisure—and operate the machinery all by themselves? As the microwave made its *feep* noise, signalling completion, she added mentally, *Or that I would be able to thaw four pounds of beef in fifteen minutes?*

Dennis was right on time; the doorman buzzed while the griddle was heating. "Please send him up, Osvaldo."

"Would you like to join us for dinner?" It was a rhetorical question. Dennis's nose had visibly quivered as the scent of hash browns cooking reached it.

"Wow, yes. Thanks!"

"We're having steak and fries with a salad. Jeremy!" Connie called down the hall. "Come say hello to Dennis." The sounds of *Lady and the Tramp* stopped abruptly and her son erupted from his room. He screeched to a halt in front of Dennis and formally presented his hand for a shake.

"Well, hi, guy." Dennis shook and gave Jeremy one of those male-bonding mock punches on the shoulder that Connie always found funny. "You sure are growing fast."

Jeremy basked in the compliment and his mother realized for the thousandth time that he craved male companionship. No matter how many weekend dates he had with his father—and Bob Nathan's job and new family obligations were making them fewer and farther between—there was nothing like having a father figure home every day. *What can I do?* she asked herself, and sighed. Laughing and chattering, the boy and young man strolled together to the kitchen.

That kitchen had been the best investment she'd ever made. Most Manhattan apartments didn't have enough space to swing a cat and the idea of eating in the same room where you cooked was laughable. This place had been no exception when she'd first seen it, but next to the kitchen had been a maid's room. As Connie had said to the real-estate agent, "No way am I ever going to have a live-in maid, unless I hold up a bank!" So the wall between the two rooms had come down and now there was space for a comfy dining area plus the double-size freezer that was the key to her cooking style.

Before seating himself, Dennis politely asked permission and then fastidiously removed his jacket. "Sharp suit," his hostess noted. Connie let him polish off two slabs of beef and start on a third before she got down to business. "So, Dennis, what's the dirt on the Marquise de Vernay?" Belatedly, she realized that if it really was dirt he couldn't tell it in front of a seven-year-old.

"Fascinating!" Her assistant wiped his mouth neatly and Jeremy copied him. "I thought there wouldn't be a whole lot of information available because, you know, there's been no news about her in recent years. But it turns out she was a real headline-grabber when she was young."

"No kidding! Eat some more salad, Jeremy." She turned back to Dennis. "Do tell."

"Well, her debut was one of the biggest social occasions of 1910. The Carmodys went all-out to launch their little girl. There was a ball at their mansion—where you're working—that was said to cost a quarter of a million dollars. And that's when a dollar really was a dollar. One of the highlights was a row of one hundred and ten liveried footmen lining both sides of the staircase, holding silver candelabra to light the debutante's entrance."

"You should see those stairs now," Connie rejoined drily. "But it must have been quite a sight."

"So was Augustine. Really lovely, I've got photos."

"I've seen one of them, and that's what piqued my interest. How did such a sweet-looking girl turn into such a nut case?"

"Bad taste in men." Dennis laughed. "After she made her debut, Miss Augustine Carmody was the belle of the ball for the whole social season. All the eligible guys were chasing her like mad because, in addition to being the sole heir to the fortune, she was also the prettiest millionairess in town. Everybody liked her, too. She wasn't spoiled or anything. The papers were full of rumors about the marriage proposals she got. There was one from a Vanderbilt—I forget the first name—and some English duke with a big castle but no money. But she turned them all down and fell in love with Harry Cheney."

"Elbows, J, elbows," Connie reminded her son, who had both of them parked on the table. "I remember that name from the obit. Who was Cheney?"

"He was bad news. Came from a blueblooded Virginia family but they had cut him off after some trouble in university. He married a gal from Montana who had inherited a silver mine and she died in a suspicious riding accident just seven months after the wedding."

"What do you mean, suspicious? Was this guy a murderer?"

"That's what everybody thought," Dennis answered, nodding. "But they couldn't prove it, so he got her money. He moved to New York and became famous for chasing showgirls and losing big amounts at card games. He'd spent pretty much everything when he wangled an invitation to meet Augustine Carmody."

The tale got sadder and sadder. Reading over the file after Dennis left, Connie found herself actually feeling sorry for the late Marquise. She hoped Kenneth Considine would share her sympathy and could hardly wait to talk to him the next morning. In fact, why didn't she just phone him right now?

Resist! she told herself firmly. *Resist being so obvious.* Besides, what would she do if a *woman* answered his phone? Augustine's story would keep.

BUT IT CAME BUBBLING out of her and into Ken's ears even before Fitch had the mansion's front door open the next morning. By the time they had gotten to the second floor she was up to "They got married and apparently everybody but Augustine knew that Cheney was keeping a girlfriend in an apartment just a few blocks from their house. From *this* house," Connie corrected herself.

"Aw." Ken looked genuinely pained, she was glad to observe. "What a rotten guy."

"Rotten to the core, as the saying goes. But Augustine soon had a son who was her pride and joy. She was so oblivious to what was going on that she named him Harry Cheney, Junior. That's the painting in the bedroom, remember, the tacky one? Her little boy."

"So it wasn't a work of art, it was a memento."

"Right. Then one fine day in the Roaring Twenties, Harry and his lover apparently skipped town. They were never seen again and neither were the millions of dollars he'd siphoned out of his wife's bank accounts. Literally millions!"

"How did he get away with it?" Ken was so aghast that he stopped examining the small etching which had caught his eye just at five o'clock the day before.

"In those days a husband had automatic access to his wife's assets. But Augustine and her family caused a real ruckus about it—so much so that there was a reform of the state's banking laws. To this day, it's known as The Cheney Ruling."

"And then?" he prompted.

"Then the abandoned Mrs. Cheney waited the statutory seven years and had her husband declared legally dead. But in the meantime their boy died of pneumonia. I'm guessing, but I think that painting was a posthumous portrait."

"Sad." Ken seemed genuinely touched.

"Anyway, she married that Italian duke, d'Urso. But by that time the scandal and loss of her baby had made her a little weird. Reclusive. Her friends gradually stopped sending invitations because she seldom went out, and when she did, she took to wearing veils and disguises. She'd also started buying things. In his divorce complaint, the duke cited...wait a minute." Connie rummaged through Dennis's folder for the copy of a faded clipping. "Yeah, here it is. He talked about her 'wanton dispersal of capital' as proof that Augustine was mentally unbalanced. Then the creep demanded a big cash settlement to let her go! But our girl really hit her stride during the Depression."

"Smart," Ken noted approvingly. "In the thirties art prices sank down to nineteeth-century levels—less than half of what they had been during the boom years. I'll bet she got some terrific bargains, maybe including this." He held up the etching for Connie's perusal. It appeared to be the design for a much larger painting and showed the Holy Trinity accepting a saint into heaven.

"Elegant. I'd almost guess—Tiepolo?"

"Bingo!" Ken beamed at her. "It *is* Tiepolo and first-rate, at that. Excuse my interruption. What about the last husband, Vernay?"

"That's even sadder. It wasn't a love match at all. The only thing they seemed to share was a passion for collecting. He had the expertise and contacts and she had the moola. The press acted very, very surprised when they tied the knot. They kept referring to the Marquise as a 'confirmed bachelor,' which is . . ."

"The polite way of saying 'homosexual,'" Ken finished her sentence. She had noticed that happening more and more between them lately. He would start to say something and just let it trail off, knowing she understood, or vice versa. "So the pretty girl in the photo turned into a bitter, misanthropic old woman."

"It's kind of like a fairy tale," Connie mused solemnly. "I've been reading them to Jeremy at bedtime. Here we've got a beautiful young princess, great wealth, a castle and a villain—and a sad ending. You'd be surprised at how many fairy tales are like that. I didn't remember unhappy endings from when I was a child."

"I know what you mean." He was looking at her with a pensive expression. "Sad endings are a grown-up thing."

Her heart leaped into her throat and seemed to stick there. Was it possible? Was Ken vulnerable, too? Was he vulnerable to *her*? For a few moments, time was suspended as they gazed at each other; she knew she would remember and cherish that moment for the rest of her life.

But before Connie could summon the courage to say something, to make a gesture of commitment, the connection snapped, the opportunity passed. They went back to their labors and that night she told Jeremy the "fairy tale" about Augustine de Vernay. Mother and son agreed that it was a sad, sad story. Tucking the boy in, she couldn't help wondering "Am I going to end up like her, alone, except for my son? Will I ever be able to break through the wall of reserve that surrounds *my* prince?"

But then Jeremy's contribution to the Vernay project bore fruit and she had a lot more to think about.

7

SPRING HAD FINALLY, reluctantly, gloriously arrived in Manhattan. Trees flowered on the Vernay mansion's lawn. The uniformed guards gladly shed their heavy overcoats to reveal tailored tunics, except for Fitch who was always fastened up to the neck—even his dog looked well-groomed at all times. She and Ken no longer shivered their way through the house each day.

They had almost finished itemizing the top stories of the stone hulk. Behind them, in their wake, each room and its contents was clean and orderly though still jam-packed. Every object of merit bore a tag with a catalogue number, its supposed history—known in the art field as "provenance"—and estimated value. A second tag indicated whether the team thought the thing should make its way to the galleries of the New York or the auction block at Villiers, Buck.

Windows were opened and fresh air made the house feel cleaner, more alive. Even better, Connie no longer was compelled to make a beeline for the shower the instant she got home. They had made such progress that a person could walk through any of the bedrooms or upstairs halls without dodging a possible avalanche of treasure.

The only unexplored space on the second floor was a linen closet near the head of the stairs. "At least, I think it's a linen closet," she said in exasperation after they opened the door and viewed the jumble inside. No sheets or towels were visible behind the heap of furniture and sculpture.

"More like a fancy Fibber McGee's closet," Ken added glumly. "Gee, I really thought we had finished with this floor."

It took them almost the whole day to extract, clean and record everything that was crammed into the small space. By now they had become blasé. Marble busts of Greeks and Romans, Louis XV slipper chairs, Austrian console tables—they had all become old news. After Ken had neatly vacuumed the empty closet—there *were* some old, rotting sheets on the shelves, which they used for rags—Connie did what she'd done perfunctorily in every room so far, with no results; she switched on the white metal detector and ran it up and down the walls and into corners.

The noise made both of them jump. "Beep!" went the machine. "Beep, beep, beep!" it continued more urgently as she pushed it toward the rear wall.

"Ken, do you think . . . ?" She whirled to face him as he eased into the closet. They were so close she could smell his body's alluring scent, see her reflection in the blue of his eyes.

"There's metal behind there, all right. But it could just be a steel beam."

"But the detector never made noise anyplace else."

"Hmm." In the semidarkness, Ken was peering at the shelves and wall. "I wish I'd remembered to bring a flashlight."

"Got an idea!" Connie backed out of the closet and ran down the hall to Augustine's bedroom. Sitting on top of the chest was an ugly, tarnished brass lamp—but it worked. And she remembered having screwed a hundred-watt bulb into it.

Plugged into a hall socket with its tattered shade removed, the lamp showed them that the closet's rear wall was different from the other sides. Its shelves were not nailed down but simply rested on supports. Instead of plaster, the surface was grooved wooden panels. Without a word the two of them yanked the shelves away and started tapping on the wall.

"If this was a movie," she joked nervously, "we'd suddenly hit a concealed latch and a door would swing open."

"And tumble us both into a basement dungeon." Ken laughed. "This is probably a wild-goose chase."

Several minutes of tapping, pressing and pounding yielded no results. "Maybe we should get some tools, a crowbar or something," Connie ventured halfheartedly.

"Right." He turned to go, and froze in place.

"What is it?"

Ken pointed silently. To the left of the doorway was what appeared to be an old-fashioned light switch like all the others in the house. Only the closet had no light fixture.

"I dare you!" The phrase from childhood was out of her mouth before she realized it. He grinned and punched the button. Behind them there was a solid click and a rush of stale air. The paneling had parted in the middle, like French doors. Behind it was a massive, rusty safe.

EVEN IAN BUCK sounded excited when Constance reported to him that night. "But, dear girl, however did you find the combination to open it?"

"That was almost ridiculously easy, Mr. Buck," she said, laughing. "At least, for a woman. There was a handwritten linens list tacked to the inside of the closet door. I remember my grandmother kept one, too; she was paranoid about the maid losing or stealing her precious sheets. But Augustine's list had nothing to do with the stuff that was on the shelves—the numbers were much too high. And they were the combination! All we had to do was figure out which was 'left' and which was 'right.'"

"Absolutely smashing, Constance. And what was inside?"

"Jewelry, sir, and tons of it. We were just starting to open the boxes at five o'clock when we had to leave. Believe me, I went kicking and screaming. All I had time to do was look at the names on the cases, and some of them are in Russian—Cyrillic alphabet. I picked up a Russian dictionary on my way home so I can get a handle on them tomorrow."

"Well, now, this is truly exciting. Would you say there is enough to make a full day's sale?"

Connie reviewed her mental picture of the safe as she and Ken had tugged open the heavy door. Leather, wood and metal jewel boxes completely filled the interior, which was as tall as she was. "Unless some of the cases are empty, Mr. Buck. Or some of the items aren't up to snuff . . ."

"Which has not been true heretofore, am I right?" he interrupted. "You've said *la Marquise* always bought only the best."

"Correct, sir. And based on that, I'd say we have the makings of an auction that will knock the world's socks off. Unless, of course," she added cautiously, "the New York can lay claim to a lot of it."

"Ah, yes. We must make our position quite clear with regard to this." Connie could hear the familiar, ominous steel enter her boss's voice. "Sad to say, the Museum's jewel collection is quite sparse. If we were to take only the Vernay will into consideration we might have to relinquish much of what you've found. The Russian Imperial items in particular."

She waited for the other shoe to drop; what was this wily man up to?

"But I've had our attorneys conduct a bit of research, so to speak, on the original charter of the New York. A close reading indicates the founders did not consider jewelry to be art at all and had no intention of collecting it. Thus, Mr. Considine has no claim to the contents of that safe and I shall expect to see it—in toto—in our next sales catalogue."

"I see, Mr. Buck." She swallowed nervously, envisioning her "partner's" reaction to this news.

"And, oh yes, Constance. Do keep a specially keen lookout for the Petrov diadem. As you know, it has not been seen since the late Marquise—who was still Mrs. Cheney at the time—traveled to St. Petersburg in 1929."

"Absolutely, sir." The finest platinum crown known to exist outside the British crown jewels—and she might actually see and touch it tomorrow. "If we do come upon it, I'll send one of the guards to phone you instantly. For the sake of security, the message will be, um, that we've found the documents you wanted."

"Excellent. I'll expect to hear from you." Before she could draw breath to respond, Ian Buck had hung up.

But instead of visions of gems parading through her head, what she was seeing was the face of Kenneth Considine. Who was about to get some news he would not like—from her. Her distraction—and feeling of dejection—were such that Mrs. Wickes noticed when Connie went down to pick up her son. "Is anything wrong, dear?" she asked. They were hunting through a pile of jackets and book bags to locate Jeremy's.

"Oh, Amelia," Connie sighed, "it's just that the Vernay project is turning out to be much tougher than I thought."

"And how about the gentleman from the museum?" The older woman was scrutinizing her keenly. "I understand you find him agreeable. Ken, isn't it?"

Constance gasped in dismay. "How did you know *that*?"

"Dear Jeremy has been telling us all about your search for treasure and how you speak of Ken, dear. Ah, here we are." Mrs. Wickes pulled from the heap the little navy-blue jacket with St. Barnabas's crest on the pocket; although it was only four months old it was already a bit short on the boy's wrists.

In confusion, Connie ushered her son out Mrs. Wickes's door and upstairs. She didn't know whether to be furious at him, at herself or both of the above. Had she been so screamingly, fatuously obvious? Was everybody in the building whispering that Mrs. Nathan was chasing Husband Number Two as she worked on the Vernay estate? "Just what did you tell Mrs. Wickes about Mr. Considine?" she inquired firmly over lasagna, one of her son's favorite foods.

"Who? Ken, you mean?" he replied, demolishing her attempts at ex-post-facto formality. "You talk about him all the time and he sounds real nice. And I told Mrs. Wickes you and Ken are hunting for treasure in a haunted palace."

Connie smote her forehead. "Jeremy! I completely forgot to tell you! Your metal detector—today we found a big safe hidden in the wall with it! And the safe is full of jewels, precious gems!" The rest of the meal and, indeed, the evening was devoted to telling and retelling the story of the vault and what was in it.

THE NEXT DAY dawned drizzling and gloomy, in keeping with her mood. Ken picked up on it immediately. "What's the matter, Connie?" He extended a solicitous hand to help her up the stairs.

It was her nature to be up-front and blunt, not evasive. "Ken, you and I are gonna have a battle royal today and there's nothing I can do about it. If *I* don't follow orders, then Mr. Buck will send someone else who will."

"What do you mean?" He was wary but still calm.

"Villiers, Buck and the Carmody family intend to put the jewelry—all of it—up for sale."

She expected an explosion but not as violent as it was. His amiable, charming face turned into a mask of rage. "That's bull! Pure, arrogant robbery! The New York has hardly anything like this and you know it. There probably won't be a single item in that safe that duplicates our holdings."

Connie sighed and looked at him beseechingly. "I'm not saying you're wrong. But the lawyers have gone back to the original charter of the Museum. It specifies what the institution was supposed to do, what it was to collect—paintings, sculpture, furniture and so on. Apparently there's a clause in there that can be interpreted as excluding any kind of jewelry. Mr. Buck warned me they're prepared to go to court about it."

"Oh, really?" Ken's eyes and voice had gone quite cold. Reversing himself on the stairs, he flung the words back at her over his shoulder. "Well, yours aren't the only attorneys in town."

Through the dusty windows of the front parlor, Connie could see Fitch's astonishment as the mansion's front door sprang open, impelled by a furious shove of Ken's strong shoulder. He strode across the lawn and out the gate, impervious to the guards or the rain falling on him. She figured he was headed for the phone two blocks away.

Miserably, she sat down on the staircase to await his return. She knew that, logically, the smart thing to do was open the safe by herself. She could be getting a good start on logging its contents. But the thought of it was unbearable without her partner. Not that he was going to think of *her* that way, not any more. The bond between them was broken as she'd known it would be, given their conflicting missions. But she waited anyway.

Half an hour passed before Kenneth reappeared at the front gate. From his stance, Connie could guess that rage had passed and been replaced by icy resolve. She also intuited that the New York's legal department had given him bad news. "Let's get on with it," was all he said, marching stiffly up the stairs and past her without a glance.

And "it" was real treasure in every sense of the word. Augustine de Vernay's taste in gems had been as exquisite and expensive as in all else. But unlike the rest of her acquisitions, these precious objects had been protected from dust and grime inside the vault. All Connie and Ken had to do was open the cases to see their perfection. There were gold burial amulets from ancient Egyptian graves, jeweled breastplates that once had adorned the robes of sultans, caskets and religious objects imbedded with huge, rough-cut stones in the medieval manner. There was a suite of sapphires and diamonds set in white gold—ornate, looping necklace, brooch, chandelier earrings and twin bracelets—that matched the set worn by Marie Antoinette in one of her best known portraits. Not to mention what seemed like miles of pearls, including a dog collar of baroque, pale pink orbs each the size of the last joint on Connie's thumb.

The glory went on and on—she couldn't enjoy a minute of it. Beside her, Ken was an automaton. He extracted the cases from the safe, commented professionally on what was inside them and photographed each item swiftly and efficiently. But there was no banter, no shared sense of wonder or amusement. No animation. No contact.

Even the possibility of finding the Petrov diadem failed to break his icy composure, though the whole art world had been looking for it for decades. The Princess Petrov had been cousin to the last, doomed Czar of Imperial Russia. When she saw another relative—the Grand Duchess Vladimir—wearing a custom-made tiara at court, the Princess ordered her jewelers to "Make me one like that, only better!"

The result was a series of interlocked, diamond-studded platinum circles designed to sit gracefully, yet regally on her head. Inside each circle was a little platinum hook and from each hook hung a large, precious stone. It was said that Princess Petrov had a different suite of gems for each day of the week—diamonds, rubies, emeralds, sapphires, turquoises and two sets of pearl pendants, one white and one black.

When revolution swept Russia in 1919, the Bolsheviks stormed the great palaces of St. Petersburg. The Grand Duchess Vladimir had had the wit and luck to smuggle her fabulous jewels out of the country—and then England's Queen Mary had had the good taste to buy them. Princess Petrov was not so fortunate; she barely escaped the mob with her life and spent the rest of it in genteel poverty. So while her cousin's splendid tiara adorned the royal heads of the British Empire, the Petrov diadem languished under Communist control in what was now Leningrad.

And there, the story went, the treasure-hungry Augustine Carmody Cheney pursued and bought the tiara along with many other objects. The new Soviet government was starved for cash and eagerly sold the contents of their former oppressor's palaces to anyone with the money. All anyone knew for sure was that the Petrov diadem was on view before Augustine's visit and was never seen after. "And certainly those malachite tables in the front hall must have belonged to the Czar, remember?" She was prattling on, trying to get some response from him. "They had the royal double-headed eagle crest."

"Mmm-hmm. This will be . . . Number 2113." Ken handed her a plum-colored case of Moroccan leather, which was no more or less elaborate than the twenty or so which came before. But taking it in her hands, Constance felt a shiver of premonition. It had an unusual shape, with a domed lid. And it was heavy.

Stalling for time—almost afraid, now that the moment might have come—she remarked, "No name stamped on this one. But then, a princess might not deign to have a mere tradesman's name stamped on her possessions, might she?"

Ken ignored the attempted pleasantry and kept his gaze stiffly on the catalogue page. "What are the contents?"

She closed her eyes, gritted her teeth, lifted the lid with both hands. Opened her left eye a crack. "This is it." The words came out flatly.

If the jeweler had been stymied in attempts to write anything on the exterior of the case, he had certainly made up for it inside. Set in the dome of the lid was an ebony plaque stamped in gold; without consulting the dictionary, all Connie could make out was "Petrov" and "1911." The box was lined with white satin, still pristine and sumptuous. And resting in a custom-designed nest was the Petrov diadem, dazzling Constance Fischer Nathan as it once had the Russian Imperial court. Only...

"The stones are missing!" The alarm in her voice was strong enough to make Ken look up. "The pendant jewels aren't in here!"

"Too bad." His voice dripped sarcasm. "That might really ruin the auction."

The man was impossible! Didn't he care at all that they had just solved one of the great riddles of the twentieth century? That they had seen what had been hidden from the world's eye for sixty-five years? She shouldered past him back into the safe.

It took some digging, but she located a second plum-colored case that had slipped lower in the pile. Once the front flap was lowered, it looked like a miniature chest with, yes, *seven* drawers. Holding her breath, Connie pulled the top one open. Inside were twenty-one blazing rubies.

Wordlessly, they went about photographing the Petrov diadem with its ruby suite. When she had finished hooking the stones in place and angling the tiara for Ken's camera, she excused herself and went down to the front door.

Fitch was there in a flash. "Can I help you, Mrs. Nathan? Is anything wrong?"

Did she look that dejected? How ridiculous, when she had just made such a discovery that would make her the envy of the entire art community and a good part of the world at large! "Pure fatigue, Fitch, but thanks anyway. I have a favor to ask; would you please call Mr. Ian Buck and inform him we've located the documents?"

"Located the documents. Yes, certainly." Connie tried to imagine what Ian Buck would do when he heard those words and couldn't. Resignedly, she trudged back upstairs. Ken informed her with what sounded like relish that only three of the seven drawers contained gemstones. Rubies, diamonds and white pearls were left; what had happened to the emeralds, sapphires, turquoises and black pearls they might never know.

"The Soviets may have sold them separately," she speculated without real interest. "Or they could have been stolen." It didn't matter much. Even with only three of its suites the Petrov diadem was still almost priceless. And without the chance that Kenneth Considine might ever love her, she really didn't know how she could go on.

8

"I HAVE THE FLU." It became Constance's steady alibi over the next couple of weeks when anybody asked "Why?" Why was she so depressed, so listless, so lifeless? Why couldn't she enjoy the gift Ian Buck sent her as a gesture of congratulations on locating the Petrov diadem? It was a sweet little antique Battersea porcelain keepsake box which read "Constancy is a great virtue." Why wasn't she excited about the item in *Gotham Magazine* where she was described as "The Hottest Property at Villiers, Buck"?

"I have the flu" was a lot easier than saying "My heart is broken." It was better than letting people know how the man who was supposed to be her antagonist had become her love object. And how, in doing her job, she'd destroyed any chance that that love might become real. "Flu" was much better than letting anybody know the job didn't seem to matter to her anymore.

Pretending she was physically ill rather than heartsore fended off questions from friends and fellow workers. But, alas, it could not fool Connie herself. Especially when she was in bed alone at night. That was when she cried. Come morning, it was a supreme effort to haul her body out of bed. She lashed herself into action with reminders that each day of work meant one less remaining day of torture.

And torture it was. She was up against the other side of Kenneth Considine—the stubborn man of iron principle. The man who had said those implacably hostile things about her profession when interviewed by the *Times*. The Kenneth who had turned against her and would not relent, who now spoke only when necessary and only about their work. It was agonizing to spend five days a week with this alien. Where had her dream man gone to? Where had he taken her dreams?

At least she could almost see light at the end of the Vernay tunnel. The two of them were itemizing the contents of the ground floor, so the job was more than half-completed. Another of Augustine's collecting quirks had come to light. At some point—they estimated it was in the late 1940s—she had developed a massive craving for fine oriental carpets. Kirmans, Bokharas, Beshirs, Herats and precious silken Qums. They were snapped up, rolled up and stashed wherever the Marquise could find space for them. The library alone held forty-one rugs, and photographing them posed a challenge.

They eventually had to clear the center of the room to do it. There, the first carpet was unrolled and briskly vacuumed. Then Ken climbed to the top of a stepladder for an aerial shot. The next rug was opened on top of it and this went on until the stack was almost a yard high.

Connie was writing the number card for the last one when it happened. This carpet was a particularly gorgeous Qum with an intricate medallion design and colors that shimmered like gems. She uncapped the felt-tip pen and wrote on the index card 4006. But by the time she propped the card in place the numerals were all runny.

My God! Tears were drenching the ink and she hadn't known she was crying! And now that she knew, she was unable to stop. *Keep your head down so he can't see!* she yelled inwardly. But it was no use.

"Connie? Connie? What is it?" The voice was soft and concerned and that just made it worse. She sank down on top of the stack of rugs and sobbed.

"What is it?" he repeated. He was climbing down the ladder.

"Oh, this is just pure hell!" she bawled. "You hate me and I can't stand it and it's all because of that damned jewelry!"

"I'm sorry. Really." From what she could see through her tears, he was back to looking like the Ken of old. "Sorry I've been such a bastard. I know you really didn't have any choice. It's just . . ."

"Just what?" She was digging desperately in her purse for the packet of tissues.

"Just the thought of those exquisite things and what's going to happen to them. Some ultrarich guy is going to buy them for his wife or mistress. She'll wear them—what—maybe four times a year—to fancy-dress balls that are supposed to be for charity—or party cruises on their yacht. Only a few hundred people will actually get to see them. And what they'll really be seeing is dollar signs." He was disdainful.

"What the buyer paid, you mean?"

"Right. Bucks, not beauty and artistry. While all the people who can only afford a few dollars to visit the New York will never get a glimpse of the Petrov diadem or any of it. I'll be frank with you, Connie, it makes my blood boil when great works are hidden away, locked in somebody's private vault. But I do apologize for taking it out on you." He looked sincere, contrite and totally adorable. "I know you didn't have any choice but to follow orders."

"Mmm-hmm." The sobs had almost stopped; Connie blew her nose and wiped mascara off her cheeks. *What a glamorous sight* you *must be,* she lectured herself. "If it makes you feel any better, this stuff has already been locked away for sixty-five years. And the public will be able to view it all prior to the auction."

"Not the same, but nothing I can do about it." He was rueful. "Your company does some real tough maneuvering."

"Everything about Villiers, Buck is tough," she countered wryly, going after another tissue.

"I've heard stories about Ian Buck and I should have understood the pressure you're under. I apologize again—forgive me?" When she looked up, he was holding out his hand for a conciliatory shake. She took it and a current of desire shot through her like lightning, paralyzing. Her lips parted and she was almost panting.

Their hands were locked and Ken was staring intently at her. Then, almost imperceptibly at first, she was being pulled toward him. It wasn't her arousal causing the movement, was it? No, his arm was drawing her closer. And he was smiling—smiling in a way she had never seen before. Looking down the length of his body, she could tell what the smile meant. He was fully erect, straining inside the denim of his jeans, reflecting her own desire. He saw where her eyes were focused.

"Connie?"

"Yes," she replied. He reached for her lips with his own. She reached for that glorious bulge and cupped its hardness, its size with her hand. His kiss was soft, sensuous, leisurely. He nibbled around the edges of her lips; his tongue traced their perimeter. She nibbled and licked back. His arms enfolded and supported while his hands roamed up and down her back, stroking it dreamily. She was cuddled in warmth with a heat inside her body growing and growing, becoming softer and softer in response to his strength and firmness. His left hand was inside her slacks, lazily stroking her buttock...then the right one was surrounding a breast...all the while his lips did their devilish work at the base of her throat, right where he could sense what he was doing to her pulse.

Without knowing who started it, she found herself stretching out and back on the bed of carpets topped with silk. Suddenly, Connie was in a great hurry; she was afraid she was going to climax just from his touch and it would be all over before their bodies joined. She started unbuttoning his plaid cowboy shirt and yanking it loose from his jeans at the same time. He licked the lobe of her right ear with a delicacy that brought her closer and closer.... Faster! She seized his silver belt buckle and tugged while his deft hands proceeded directly to the little clasp that fastened the front of her brassiere. Now her sweater was pulled up, her breasts loose and his head bent over them. As the hot tongue touched her right nipple it happened...her pelvis shook and bucked like a pony with the spasm....

"Damn!"

He raised his face from her breast, still sucking the nipple, and grinned, letting it go with a sucking sound. "What's the matter?"

"Well, you know... I'm sorry."

"Don't be sorry, sugar. We'll make it happen again. Let me undress you." Which he did with a finesse she'd thought impossible in a man—slipping the sweater gently over her head, sliding the bra straps down her arms. She managed to kick off her shoes while he was working on the zipper of her trousers. As he slid them down, he kissed her navel. *I've died and gone to heaven!* she giggled to herself. Then...

"Let me." He was starting to pull off his shirt but she finished the job for him, admiring the rippling muscles of his chest and shoulders. Taking a cue from his actions, she seized his left nipple gently between two teeth. He moaned and she could feel a strong pulse behind the fly of his jeans—which were the next topic. This time, taking her time, the buckle opened easily and the zipper slid down, slowed by the force of what was under it. But those cowboy boots—well, he'd gotten them off somewhere in there when she hadn't noticed.

Almost tentatively after her boldness, Connie grasped the waistband of the jeans on either side as Ken lay down and raised his hips slightly from the carpet. She pulled steadily and . . . there it was. He was a magnificent man, a stallion. Before she could admire his nakedness any longer, his arms pulled her down beside him and he was rolling over on top of her. She spread her arms and arched her body to receive him. Chest hair rubbed firmly against her nipples as he entered her smoothly, but with such a force . . .

Her last conscious thought, before her body took over completely, was—by God, he was right. *It* is *going to happen again!*

9

AND AGAIN . . . AND AGAIN. He entered and pleasured her three times. And Constance knew from his body's writhings and the little nonsense words he gasped in her ear that she had pleasured him mightily in return. After that third time, there wasn't an iota of energy left in her body. Just serenity, as they lay quietly on the silk. His head rested on her bosom and his hands were still tangled in her hair. Am I going to be able to *walk* after this? she wondered and giggled aloud.

"What is it?" Ken raised his head and propped himself on his elbows, looking down at her with a smile.

"I'm exhausted!"

The smile broadened into a grin of male self-congratulation. He bent and kissed her lightly on the lips. "Well, I'm not exactly ready to run a marathon myself. But this is the best kind of exhaustion there is."

"Mmm." She raised a hand, traced a finger down his chest to the place where it met the rug. "Have to agree with you on that." She moved her hand over to his left shoulder and ran it down an arm that had just the right amount of hair on it. Her hand ran into an obstruction—oh, a watchband. "What's the time?"

Ken pulled his fingers free of her hair and turned his hand. "Almost five," he replied casually.

Connie bolted upright. Fitch would be ringing the doorbell on the dot of five o'clock and expecting them to leave forthwith. He was a stickler for turning the burglar alarm system back on exactly when instructed. "Good grief! How long do I have?"

"Seven minutes." He sounded calm, but why not? A man could get dressed in a flash and look fine; female grooming was something else again. Grabbing her clothes and purse, she ran down the hall to a guest lavatory. Behind her, he was chuckling.

The chimes sounded as she was working on her eyeshadow. What the crying hadn't removed, the heat of lovemaking had. The light in the lavatory was no better than any place else in the mansion, so it was hard to get a smooth effect. She opened the door and found Ken standing outside, looking quite neat and rather smug. "Tell Fitch I'll be out in a couple of minutes," she hissed. He grinned and sauntered away with annoying jauntiness.

There! That was as good as it was going to get. She snapped the little case shut, shoved it back into her bag and yanked out the hairbrush, giving thanks once again to whichever deity had blessed her with a full head of strong, curly hair. After only a few quick strokes, it went from a mess to a hairdo.

Ken was standing by the front door, holding out her green suede jacket. As he helped her on with it, Connie whispered, "Nobody must know. Not a word, not a gesture."

His smile vanished, replaced by a serious look of agreement. So they departed the Vernay mansion in the same style as they had entered the morning that now seemed so long ago—acting stiffly courteous and formal. Both wished the three guards a good night and walked deliberately to the corner of Sutton Place, careful to keep a good three feet between their bodies.

"I want to talk to you," he muttered. "Dinner?"

"I'll have to call and see if Mrs. Wickes can keep Jeremy." Without a word, he fished a quarter out of his jeans and led the way to the street-corner phone.

As usual the babysitter's "Hello" was almost drowned out by the din of youthful voices at full throttle.

"Amelia, this is Connie. I would like to attend a dinner meeting that just was called. Would it be asking too much for you to . . ."

"Not at all, dear. Not at all. I always keep little extras and treats on hand for these emergencies."

Connie winced. She knew what those "treats" probably were, and they were not her idea of proper nutrition for a seven-year-old. Last time Mrs. Wickes fed Jeremy, he'd crammed down a month's ration of hot dogs, potato chips and chocolate cupcakes at one fell swoop. But one simply couldn't bring up the subject with such a wonderful woman. "Thanks so much, Amelia. You're a doll." Her gratitude was interrupted by a bloodcurdling shriek.

"Excuse me." The voice on the other end turned away but could still be heard clearly. "Paul dear, please do not hit Jason with the chair." How did she stay so calm? The voice returned. "What time do you think you'll be home, dear?"

"Oh . . . eight."

"Fine, see you then, Connie dear." Click.

"That woman is a saint!" Constance turned around and had to lower her eyes from the intensity of her lover's azure gaze. "Where do you want to go?"

"Wherever you like."

"It'll have to be someplace where nobody will know us. I mean *nobody.* Because if . . ."

He took up the awful thought and completed it. "Because if they find out about . . . us, neither the Museum or Villiers, Buck will accept our mutual judgments on the Vernay Collection."

"And both of our careers will be down the tubes," she agreed glumly. "I think we'd better go to the West Side."

They ended up at a Thai restaurant on Ninth Avenue that was nearly deserted. The ever-smiling waiter was taking their drink order—a white wine spritzer and a large Singha Beer—when she felt one of Ken's knees insinuating itself between hers. Considering the way they had spent the afternoon, it was a miracle that he still had the energy. Or that she still felt that sensual quiver inside.

Despite herself, she grinned back and, as he stretched out a hand, clasped it. "This is dangerous."

"I like living dangerously, don't you? Anyway, there's nobody here to recognize us." It was true; the only other couple in the small pine-paneled room appeared to be in their eighties and were reading the menu as if it contained the secrets of the universe.

"Well, we'll have to be really, really careful from here on out." Lord, had she really said that? Now she was propositioning him! "I mean...I mean...if we..." The hot sensation in her cheeks meant the blush must be visible. *Damn.*

"Yes, we'll be careful." He was still grinning. "But that doesn't mean we can't have . . . fun. After all, we've got the most secure little hideout in the world."

It was true, she realized with a jolt, but her mind hadn't gotten that far yet. And it sounded as if it came from a man with considerable sexual and romantic experience. Once again, her mouth was uttering what her brain yelled "Don't ask!" To wit, "How come you never got married?"

Ken laughed so hard the table shook and the waiter couldn't put down their drinks. The old couple turned at the noise, stared incuriously and went back to their reading. "That's what I like about you, Connie. No games, no nonsense. You just come right out with it."

"Because I'm an idiot, that's why!" She rocked her head in her hands. "Please forgive me for prying."

Still smiling imperturbably, the waiter served the wine and beer. Ken raised his glass. "Cheers. And it's certainly not prying, not after this afternoon." The knee between hers wiggled suggestively. "But as a matter of fact, I did get married."

Fortunately, her mouth was full of wine and couldn't commit another moronic blunder right away. Was the

Shaker Heights story just a false rumor? She swallowed and raised eyebrows politely. "Oh, really?"

"I was at the University of Louisville—my family's from a little town thirty miles east of there. Farmers, really, though my father considered himself an inventor. We were always broke. Luckily for me, I managed to get a couple of scholarships to pay the tuition."

"Two? I'm impressed."

"Well, only one was for brains. The other one—" he looked a little sheepish "—was for playing football."

"What position were you?"

"Quarterback, only I never actually played a college game. During the third week of practice a couple of linebackers collided and I was stupid enough to be in between them. I've got five bolts in my left thigh and the doctors advised me to stay off the gridiron if I wanted to walk normally for the rest of my life."

"Ouch!" She winced.

"Ouch is right. I was never really crazy about football anyway. It was just one of *many* attempts to get out of a small town and into the big world. Realistically speaking, I never thought a major in art history would do it."

"So you were at the University..." she prompted.

"Right. That's where I met Lacey. Lacey McCally. She was everything a boy from Alton Station, Kentucky could dream of. Blond, pretty and rich. I was crazy about her." He grimaced in remembered pain. "And she seemed to be crazy about me. So we ran off and got married the middle of sophomore year."

"Wow, you were really young."

"Young and dumb." Ken smiled sardonically.

"She didn't really care for you?"

"Oh, she cared for me just fine as long as I did exactly as she wanted and let her arrange my life. Turned out she was supremely uninterested in college as anything but a place to find her ideal mate. And that ideal was some guy who would fit smoothly into her family, go to work for her rich daddy and eventually take the helm of his company."

Connie could imagine how well industry would suit somebody as devoted to his calling as Kenneth Considine. "What kind of business was it?"

"That's the best part." He grinned. "The McCally Corporation was a leading manufacturer of what they call 'keepsakes and commemoratives.' The year I married Lacey, their big item was an Elvis lamp. The bulb was in Elvis's microphone."

She had to laugh at the image it conjured up. Ken, the worshipper of Rembrandt and Raphael, the expert on Corot and Caravaggio! She thought of him contemplating a ceramic Elvis Presley, wearing one of his spangled jumpsuits, no doubt, with a lighted mike, and kept on laughing.

"It wasn't even a *good* Elvis." Now he was chuckling along with her. "Looked more like Roy Orbison to me. But Daddy McCally had big plans for the lamp and Lacey had big plans for me. Right after we tied the knot, she dropped out of school and ordered me to switch from art history to the Business School. That was so I'd have the managerial skills to make Elvises and plastic Jesuses for the dashboard." The tone had turned bitter again. He stopped.

"You would have been miserable. How long did it last?"

"She walked out on me when she realized I wasn't going to change my major—four months. And I thought she loved me."

"How awful!"

Ken rubbed his chin reflectively. "Yeah, it was awful, all right. The only escape I had was to get deeper and deeper into my studies and take a couple of outside jobs so I had no time to think about it. But that led to a whole new kind of problem."

Was he leading up to the Miss Shaker Heights story? *Be subtle, Stupid!* she warned herself. "What do you mean?"

"When I was in Cleveland, at the Ardsley, I met a girl. And I did to her exactly what my ex-wife did to me—assumed she would go along with *my* life plan without asking her. We were even engaged. I got a feeler from the New York about this job. Came here, interviewed and accepted the position without saying a single word to her. And it never occurred to me that I was being self-centered! I felt like a real heel."

"What did she do when she found out?"

"What she had every right to do. Told me I was a rat, that she was going to stay right there in Cleveland and that I should go straight to hell." He looked rueful but far from brokenhearted.

"The New York was your ultimate goal, am I right?"

"Absolutely. This museum has been my dream ever since I read about it in the old *Life* magazine, and that's when I was in fifth grade. When push came to shove, the job was more important to me than my personal life was. Now, what's your story?"

Gulp. Just as she was planning to probe the job-versus-love-life issue a bit more deeply, he had neatly turned the tables. "Less dramatic than yours, I guess. Born and brought up right here and I went to NYU—New York University. I minored in art history, but my father talked me into going after a business degree. He firmly believed that anyone with an MBA would get rich—and that all art historians end up living in garrets and wearing secondhand clothes."

Ken laughed. "I'll bet he told you to 'be realistic' about career choices."

"You've got it. So I went to B-school and that's where I met Bob—Bob Nathan, my ex. We got married right after we finished school."

"What went wrong?"

"Aw—Bob's a real nice guy. We're still good friends and he was a total gentleman about the divorce. It's just . . . we wanted completely different things in life."

"Which are . . . ?"

Connie shrugged. "Bob *loves* the big-money scene, investment banking. And he's real good at it. But you're expected to work twenty-hour days and think about nothing but the business at all times. I tried a couple of years and hated it, even after I got promoted. We're talking total loathing."

"So you quit?"

"Well, Jeremy came along and rescued me," she chuckled. "I took maternity leave and never went back."

"How did you ever get into Villiers, Buck? That is—" he cleared his throat, obviously trying to be tactful "—you're not their stereotypical executive."

"You mean I'm not a British guy with a title that goes back to Ethelred the Unready? Yeah, I've noticed that. I sort of got in the back door, through the money side. Mr. Buck had realized that the company's financial department was still stuck in the nineteenth century, maybe the eighteenth century. There were all these bookkeepers sitting at rows of desks recording everything manually! No central computer, no cash-flow tracking and absolutely no idea of what our resources actually were."

"Museum staffs tend to be like that too," Ken nodded. "The accounting department in Louisville reminded me of something out of Dickens."

Connie laughed. "Exactly! So V-B was looking for someone with a financial background and at least a nodding acquaintance with art and antiques. It was perfect timing—Jeremy had just started nursery school. And most of the people they interviewed wouldn't take the job because it sounded as if it would be temporary, a short-term thing. After the financial department was restructured there wouldn't be anything to do."

"You're still there." He squeezed her hand.

"Yes, while I was shaking things up a couple of auctioneers found out that *my* predictions of what a sale would yield were closer than the professionals'. Mr. Buck heard about it and made me an Assistant Director. *Et voilà,*" she finished with a flourish, "there you have my life story."

"Except you got divorced," Ken reminded her.

"Oh, yes." Somberly. "Well, as time went on, the job made more and more demands on me. Bob didn't like that—he was used to calling me in to help with research on a corporate acquisition, or bringing a couple of guys home to dinner on short notice. The blowup came when I was assigned a scouting trip to Europe the same week his company was buying out an aircraft manufacturer. When the yelling stopped, we agreed it just wasn't working out. That was two years ago and he's already remarried. I feel badly for Jeremy, but . . ."

Connie stopped her narrative when beef *saté* and pepper chicken with coconut milk arrived via the waiter. They ate in comfortable silence, his knee still wedged between hers. She ached to ask "What happens now?" but kept her peace.

In the taxi, going up West End Avenue, Ken took her in his arms again for a slow, deep kiss that seemed to make time stop. She only opened her eyes when the car came to a halt.

"That'll be four-fifty," the driver said. Through the partition she could see he was smiling at them.

"I'm going on to the East Side," Ken responded.

Her heart sank at the thought of parting, but it would be fatal if he came upstairs. It was already past eight and Jeremy would be waiting impatiently. And what if the neighbors—including Amelia Wickes—saw him and put two and two together? Meekly, she let Ken open the door for her and got out of the cab.

"See you tomorrow," he said formally.

"Yes, good night," she responded in kind for their unseen audience. And then jumped a bit as she realized that he'd managed to glide his hand sexily across her bottom as she passed.

Jeremy was already in bed when she thought to check the answering machine in the kitchen. "Mrs. Nathan, this is Whatley," it said brusquely. Good grief, Ian Buck's butler! She had forgotten to call her boss with the daily report!

"Whatley, this is Constance Nathan. Please tell Mr. Buck that I had a family emergency and do apologize for not phoning sooner.... Everything's all right now, thank you.... No, we are still in the library, working on the carpet collection... I will call tomorrow. Good night."

The questions she hadn't asked Ken came back to haunt her at bedtime. Such as—what's next for us? Is this just a sexual thing? He seemed so sympathetic and sincere but what healthy male would turn down the opportunity? And the man she'd seen when he was angry about losing the jewels was a different character altogether, extremely tough-minded. Not to mention that he'd supplied plenty of proof that the most important thing in his life was his work, not his woman. And that she would have to conduct an elaborate charade to conceal all signs of their sexual involvement.

"You've really done it this time, Constance," she said to the ceiling. And promptly fell asleep.

10

"GOOD MORNING, FITCH."

"Good morning, Mrs. Nathan. You look like you finally shook off that flu bug."

What? Oh, yes. "You're quite right, thanks. It's wonderful to feel human again." Constance laughed. "And what a glorious day!" She and the dignified guard admired the clear blue sky reflected in the river, the spring-green lawn and violets blooming even in the long-neglected Vernay gardens.

They were waiting for Kenneth Considine to arrive. The rules were that the team had to sign in—and enter the house—together. But nine o'clock came and went with no trace of her new lover. Unbidden and unreasonable, a cold edge of alarm shivered through her body. No, of course, he couldn't have skipped out. He had a job to do! But until now, hadn't he arrived every day between 8:30 and 8:45? He was a stickler for promptness, she knew.

"This is not like Mr. Considine," Fitch offered at 9:20.

"No, indeed." She was grateful for the opening. "Maybe I'd better try calling him."

It was an effort to walk calmly, at a reasonable pace, until she turned the corner on Sutton Place and Fitch couldn't see her anymore. She fumbled for a quarter with hands that were shaking in a most adolescent manner. The phone in Ken's apartment rang six, seven, eight times before she gave up. She punched 411 for information; "Could you give me the number for the Executive Offices of the New York Museum of Art?"

She was muttering "Eight—two—six—three—five hundred" over and over, rummaging in the bottom of her bag for another quarter. A tap on the shoulder startled her so much that she almost dropped it. "Eek!" came out squeakily before she spun—and saw the tap had come from the object of her calls.

Ken was panting slightly and rubbing the thigh she now knew held five metal bolts. "What happened?"

"Did you know the President is in town?" He was angry but not at her.

"Uh, yeah, I guess."

"Well, he decided to have breakfast at the Hotel Carlyle this morning."

Connie slumped with relief and enlightenment. Anybody born and bred in Manhattan would immediately know the whole story; the swank Carlyle was just a few blocks from Ken's apartment. And, naturally, the police and Secret Service would have closed off Madison Avenue to safeguard the Chief Executive's motorcade. "That must be some traffic jam."

"Unbelievable!" His arms waved, describing total chaos. "I decided to try the subway and must have read the map wrong. Next thing I knew, I was at a station called Astor Place."

She smothered a laugh—he'd taken an express train by mistake and been carried miles south of Sutton Place. "Good thing you got off there. Next stop would have been Brooklyn."

Still grumpy, he eyed the phone kiosk. "Who were you calling?"

"You. We were worried." The use of "we" was a good cover. Wouldn't want him to think she was a clinging female. Heading back to the mansion, she chatted with feigned casualness. Ken retold his tale to Fitch, who managed to keep a straight face, and then they were in the house again. In the library with the silken carpet that had plunged her into tears and then ecstasy.

As if reading her mind, he bent for a soft kiss. "I guess we'd better get cracking," he murmured, drawing away from her lips with obvious reluctance.

"Mmm." She was equally unwilling. "If we fall behind schedule, slow down the pace, they'll notice."

Ken groaned comically. "I can imagine the temper tantrum Emilio would throw."

So could Constance. Emilio Sant'Angelo, the director of the New York Museum of Art, was almost as famous for his explosions as for his fanatical attention to detail. He had once, personally, torn up hundreds of leaflets for a Museum show on the Emperors of Rome. "Domitian's ears are *wrong!* All wrong!" he'd screamed at the hapless illustrator. But Sant'Angelo's rages didn't last, and everybody knew he was really softhearted. He had never, ever fired a single employee . . . unlike Ian Buck.

The thought of her boss was galvanizing. "What shall we tackle next?" She edged around the plateau of rugs to get a closer look at the wall, which was hung from floor to ceiling with paintings. Down at knee level there was a smallish one, barely two feet square, that somehow caught her eye. It needed cleaning badly, but glorious color shone through the grime.

The scene was a Victorian family picnicking at the edge of a grove, the women shielded by parasols and stiff in their whalebone corsets. Yet it filled the viewer with a sense of ease and serenity. "Manet?" she ventured to her partner.

Ken took the direct way across the room. He crawled over the carpets and lay down on his stomach for an eye-level view of the little work. "Hmm," he mused intently. "Certainly the subject matter and brushwork are characteristic. But the palette is rather different from..."

The professorial talk went on but the words failed to register. Hunkered down by the wall, she admired this man again as she had at their first meeting. His face was such a terrific combination of masculine ruggedness and sensitivity—the softness of eyes, lashes and lips counterpointed by high cheekbones and square chin.

"Considering the condition and that overlay of decaying varnish, I'd have to take a closer look in the laboratory before I could say for sure whether it's a true Manet or from a lesser hand. A student, perhaps." Now Ken had turned and was meeting her gaze. His lecture trailed off and led smoothly to another kiss. But this one was not broken off by talk of duty and work. Instead, his hands fastened on her shoulders and pulled Connie slowly but irresistibly onto the jewel-toned rug, their bed of pleasure.

Today she was not too dazed, too astonished to relish and remember every moment and movement of his love-play, her eyes wide open until almost the very end. She could see the effects of her own ministrations—the way a soft bite at the base of the neck set him to shuddering and how he moaned unknowingly when she moved beneath him just so. She took it all in, from the tan line on the back of his neck—weekend skiing at Sugarbush—to the horrific scar on the thigh that marked the end of his football career. And his body, his lovemaking, were all unutterably sweet and heart-wrenchingly perfect.

Which, of course, is what's making me so nervous, she thought when they were done and lying peacefully once more on the silk, their bodies still entwined. How can he be this wonderful and still available? "Where," as my grandmother said whenever anybody offered her a "deal," "is the catch?"

"Remember the time—" now it was Grandmother's voice speaking clearly inside her head "—when you found that taffeta dress down on Orchard Street, Constance? The gray-and-pink gown that was just like the one in Saks but at *one-third* the price? Remember, young lady, how I said 'Where's the catch?' And you said, 'It only has a little spot on it. I'll send it to the cleaners.' But dry cleaning showed the dress had really been pink and white. And no matter what we did, that stubborn gray spot was right there on the bodice."

Yes, I remember, Connie told the ghost of her mother's mother. So where's the catch here? Where is the gray spot on Kenneth Robert Considine, once married, once divorced, once engaged and still available?

She raised her head and noted with a grin that the object of her wonder was fast asleep. His arm resting across her breasts and a leg wedged between hers made a silent exit impossible. "Ken!" she whispered and watched his eyelids flutter. "It's almost eleven-thirty."

That did it. He bolted upright and, as before, looked immaculate by the time she returned from the lavatory. The camera and tripod were set up facing the picnic scene. He was consulting the catalogue—actually, it was their third. Two of the giant tomes were already full. "What number are we up to?"

"Four thousand and seven." She knew that without having to look at the book; the Qum carpet was forever engraved in her mind as 4006. "I'll bet we crack the seven-thousand mark by the time we're through."

"Mmph," he grunted in assent, squinting through the viewfinder. "Still won't be the biggest collection ever—not even close to Warhol's. I'm getting some glare on the upper left corner, please."

Connie adjusted the light, frowning. "Oh, that's an unfair comparison!" She was, oddly, feeling protective of Augustine and her trove. "For one thing, most items in Warhol's house were listed individually. We're cataloguing everything that matches—china or crystal or whatever—under a single number. That better?"

"Fine, thanks."

As the lens clicked she pursued her train of thought. "And anyway, none of these are cookie jars." It was true; executors of Andy Warhol's estate had found his town house crammed with everything from Egyptian funerary urns to 1940s American kitchenware. The public had snapped it all up at record prices. Still, to traditionalists like Connie and Ken, it was clear that the Marquise de Vernay had collected on a higher plane. She bought nothing whose merit and credentials had not been confirmed by at least a century of expert scrutiny.

"Maybe a cookie jar would be kind of a relief." Once finished shooting the possible Manet, he was grinning again. "I'm getting sort of jaded by all this perfection—present company included."

Laughing, she acknowledged the compliment. "Likewise, sir, likewise. How do we tag it?"

Ken closed one eye and squinted at the little picnic scene. "For this one, I don't even have to look in our book. If you're right and it *is* Manet, our Impressionist gallery already has seventeen of them and is bursting at the seams. If it's just the work of a student, Emilio and the Trustees won't want it." He imitated an auctioneer banging his gavel on the podium at the end of a bidding round. "Sold! To Villiers, Buck. Even though I hate to see it go."

"Yes, it's quite sweet no matter who painted it." Connie bent her head as she wrote out the appropriate tag designations: 19th cent. Eur.—for European—poss. Manet? Lab Inspection required. Value undetermined. She felt in her bones that this work was the real thing and that she'd just scored a real coup. Wouldn't want it to show on her face. Second tag: To Villiers, Buck. Appraisal/inspection immediately.

Ken docilely taped the two tags to a corner of the picture's frame and edged his tripod two feet to the left. "Here, however, we have another case altogether." His tone was smooth—too smooth. "Because this, my dear girl, is a Van Eyck."

"Aargh!" The strangled cry was all she could get out. No wonder he'd been so calm about losing an Impressionist! A fifteenth-century Flemish master was worth ten times as much and hardly ever came on the market. Glumly, she peered at the painting of a rather strict-looking angel visiting a shaven-pated monk in his austere cell. "You're sure?"

"Yup." He was dusting it off with a soft brush and a possessive air. She knew what was coming next. "And if you'll consult the records, ma'am, you'll see that there exists a certain gap in our Northern Renaissance holdings. A definite, beautiful gap—which is now being filled."

"Ha-hah." With as much grace as possible she arranged lights on either side of the rather grim painting. Of course, he was right. She could now see all the signposts of the Flemish School—microscopic brush strokes, dense detail and those soft, white, late-medieval bodies. Seduced by the easy charm of the picnic painting, her eye had passed over this masterwork from a far earlier epoch. "I'll take your word for it."

"Thanks. And don't worry, Connie. No matter what kind of tricks Buck put you up to, we'd get this one."

FORTUNATELY FOR HER, Ian Buck reasoned the same way. With trepidation, she delivered the tale about the Van Eyck in her nightly phone report. "Where do you suppose the Marquise managed to get her hands on it?" she asked the Englishman.

"The Russians, I imagine." He sounded bitter but not angry. "We've heard stories about several Flemish works vanishing from the Imperial palaces before the Soviets managed to reestablish order. Pity to see this one slip away."

"Sir, I went through both our books..."

"Of course, of course." He was curt. "Couldn't be helped."

She had carefully saved the good news for the end. "On the upside, Mr. Buck, we've got ourselves what I'm pretty sure is a Manet—and topflight." To his enthusiastic queries, she responded with a detailed description of the painting—plus an exaggerated version of her own guile in hiding from Considine how sure she was of its authenticity.

"Well done, Constance! We've had superb demand for Impressionists lately, as you know." This was certainly true. Auction prices for these warm, emotional works of art had been skyrocketing for the past decade. Cynics in the art community commented that the newly rich and insecure felt comfortable with this "pretty" style. And anyway, its range of colors was so easy to *decorate* around. "I believe I shall let several of our good friends in on this little secret."

Connie knew that "good friends" was a euphemism for "hot customers with lots of cash." "Excellent idea, sir. To help build the excitement."

"Precisely. Well, good night, Constance." As usual, he hung up so swiftly she couldn't reply.

But the kitchen phone surprised her by ringing again. "Hello?"

The nearness and sensuality of the voice took her breath away. "I just wanted to wish you good night and sweet dreams."

"Oh! Good night, Ken." She bit her lip to keep from adding "Darling."

11

"FISH!"

"Bird!"

If anyone other than Barbara Hollobird Salter had called her "Fish," Constance would have killed with pleasure. But instead she hugged her old friend gleefully. Their respective nicknames dated back to freshman year at Miss Whitney's when the style was to go by a mutant version of one's family name. "Fischer" and "Hollobird" made it easy.

"Wow, you look terrific!" Barbara marvelled, stepping back for a head-to-toe survey. "The art world seems to be agreeing with you."

"Hey, thanks. You're looking pretty nifty yourself. Much more relaxed and rested. Is that Florida or just the kids getting bigger?"

"Both. And Dick's out from under all that pressure, too." Barbara Hollobird had married Richard Salter right after graduation from NYU. She took a job in Syracuse to help put him through Cornell's School of Hotel Management. Thereafter, the couple had hopscotched across the country, as Dick moved up the corporate ladder of the giant Sceptre Hotel organization. Barbara produced two boys and two girls, born in San Antonio, Kansas City, New Orleans and Chicago. In that last city, Dick got a long-awaited promotion to assistant manager of the huge Shoreline Sceptre overlooking Lake Michigan. He and his wife believed their years of nomadic living would finally be rewarded.

But the job was not what they had hoped; Dick was overworked, under constant stress, with little time for his family. When Constance had last visited her old friend, "Bird" was pale, thin and frazzled from coping with four small kids and bolstering an unhappy spouse.

Now Barbara was tanned and sun had lightened her long blond twist of hair. After two years of struggle in Chicago, she and Dick had agreed that their life together was more important than a lofty managerial position. Dick had requested assignment to a smaller establishment and was now managing a small Sceptre retreat on Longboat Key, off the coast of Sarasota. Constance also noted with familiar envy that the weight Barbara had regained had gone straight to her bosom.

"I'm so happy for you." She took her friend's arm to steer her into the main room of Venezia Azzuro. "And I'm really sorry we couldn't pop over for a visit on the way home from Disney World. I had to pay a visit to a client in Palm Beach and Jeremy had to be back in school that Wednesday."

"Next time," Barbara replied, scanning the room in open awe. "Jeez, Fish, this sure is swanky." Even on a Saturday afternoon the restaurant was packed with the beautiful, the chic and the merely rich. The smell of money, power and intrigue was as thick in the air as the aroma of Italian haute cuisine.

Tino glided suavely up to the two women. "Mrs. Nathan! Always such a pleasure."

You're not kidding, pal, Connie answered silently. Villiers, Buck insisted that their representatives should always have the best tables in the house; so they authorized generous Christmas presents and regular emoluments for Tino and the maitre d's at a number of other top-notch eateries. "This is my old friend, Mrs. Salter."

"Enchanted." Tino clicked his heels and bowed, eyes sweeping almost imperceptibly over Barbara's lush bustline. "This way, if you please."

Crossing the room, Connie paused twice to chat with clients and give them the "inside scoop" on the Vernay Collection. This, of course, was why the auction house cheerfully shelled out thousands and thousands of dollars in expense money to her and its other sales executives. Every contact with a possible buyer, every little talk with a wealthy, acquisitive collector built interest in what Villiers, Buck had to sell. As Connie doled out snippets of gossip with a "Please don't pass this on"—but of course they would—she made her listeners feel that they were insiders, privy to secret information, ahead of the crowd.

"Why, Mr. Wirthel, so nice to see you back in town. Mrs. Wirthel, that turnout is divine. Pardon? Well, we are still slogging through the Vernay mansion. The size of the collection is staggering, simply staggering. And it is all—I was going to say 'first-rate' but that would be an understatement. It is absolutely topflight, every single item. Just between you and me—" *lean a little closer and lower the voice,* "—her Impressionist collection is *not* as extensive as we'd expected. But there is a little Manet in the library, a picnic scene that . . ." She interrupted her sentence to bunch her fingers together and kiss their tips in the Italian gesture that means "perfection!"

The Wirthels, naturally, now had their hearts set on the Manet and would bid for it vigorously. Connie's second stop was at the table of the Belgian industrialist Théodore de Mayère and his mistress. Baron de Mayere had the tact not to appear publicly with her on the Continent, where his wife was a social luminary. But America is a different place altogether, no?

"Congratulations on your polo victory in Argentina, Baron! Mademoiselle, was that your cottage in Southampton that we saw in *Architectural Digest*? So elegantly understated . . . Mmm-hmm, you know how *I've* been spending my time... Ah, sir, I would say that both the Museum and Villiers, Buck can expect an embarrassment of riches." *Good thing you remembered that the Baron's sister is on the Board of the New York, Constance.* "No, I don't believe the exact sale dates have been set yet. But I have a strong feeling—" this was the signal for leaning close and whispering "—that for anyone interested in certain mysteriously missing Russian Imperial jewelry, this will be a *fascinating* autumn!" *Laugh.* "No, no! I can say no more! Perhaps a chat with Mr. Buck . . . ?" Her boss would love that. "Such a pleasure to see you again."

"What the hell was all that?" Barbara muttered as they were seated. The table was indeed a choice one, on the room's elevated section right next to the railing. Perfect for seeing and being seen.

"That was business." It was a relief to talk normally again. She had mastered the arch conversational style of High Society, but it was not comfortable. "I was drumming up interest in the Vernay Collection."

"What's that?" Constance's mouth dropped open in astonishment for a moment. Then she had to laugh at herself. "Oh, God, I've gotten so into this job that I forget what the real world is like!" The creations of long-dead artists and artisans amassed by a rich old lady now dead herself would not be the epicenter of fascination for a farmer in Kansas, a teacher in Oregon or a hotelier on the Gulf of Mexico. Starting from the beginning, Connie did her best to describe for her friend what Augustine de Vernay had done and what her estate meant to the wealthy international community that circled through Manhattan's art scene. Not to mention what the Vernay Collection meant to the career of Constance Fischer Nathan.

"Aha, I see. You've been promoted," Bird said, nodding enthusiastically.

"Right. And today I'm feeling specially good because I'm dressed like a civilized person for a change." Day after working day of jeans-and-sneakers in the dirty mansion had created a strong itch to be chic.

When she'd found out that Barbara would be in town Saturday, she'd zipped out to Saks on Thursday night and scored a lavender linen suit. Well, it's the *only* thing I've bought all spring, she told her conscience soothingly. Just feel the beautiful fabric and fine tailoring in that sleeve.

"There's more to it than that." Bird was eyeing her keenly. "You're not kidding me, Fischer. You're in love."

Connie's mouth dropped open again and this time it took a lot longer to regain her composure. "For heaven's sake, keep your voice down!" was the first thing she got out.

"Aha again!" The blonde grinned fiercely. "You're not denying it, I notice."

"I should have known. You always could read me like a book. Shhh!" Constance warned as the busboy approached. With ceremony, he placed crystal glasses of ice water on the table, then little pots of sweet butter and a silver basket lined with white linen. The basket was piled high with the feathery-light rolls that were a trademark of Venezia Azzuro.

Following the busboy was the waiter, pad in hand. "What do you suggest?" Bird asked.

"Bellinis are a must here. Am I right, Eduardo?"

"Completely so, Mrs. Nathan. Two Bellinis it will be."

"It's the latest drink," Connie explained. "Champagne and peach juice—it looks almost as good as it tastes."

"Quit stalling."

Where to start? How to tell the story? "First thing, Bird, you've got to swear not to tell a soul. Okay, you can tell Dick. But if this gets out, it's my neck and I'm not kidding. It could cost me my job, my whole career. God, I think I might even end up being sued by Villiers, Buck. I mean, this is serious."

Wordlessly, Barbara extended her hand for the ritual shake they'd been using to vow silence since they were thirteen years old.

"It's the guy I'm working with—the representative of the Museum. We're supposed to be deadly enemies and here I am—" Connie shrugged her shoulders helplessly.

"—in love with him," Barbara chimed in.

"'Fraid so. And if anybody finds out before the Vernay estate is divided, redistributed and auctioned, we could both get canned. I *know* I would be."

"So let's say you've cleaned out this mansion and all the stuff is in the museum or sold. What then?" Her old friend had read her mind again. That was what she dreaded contemplating.

"Well, if they heard then that we were having an affair, it wouldn't be good. But I could tell my boss that it didn't start until we had finished the job. Or—" this hurt even more "—maybe nobody would ever have to know because the whole thing would be over."

"Ouch!" Bird grimaced sympathetically. "We don't want that to happen, do we? What are his feelings, do you know?"

Connie lapsed into silence; the waiter was back with two icy champagne flutes filled with a radiant, sparkling mixture of juice and champagne. She raised her drink in a salute and sipped. "I have absolutely no idea."

The blonde's eyebrows rose. "What's he like?"

"A dreamboat, an absolute hunk!" The gates of secrecy once opened, Connie realized she'd been dying to tell somebody all about her wonderful lover. "He's smart, he's funny, he's fantastically knowledgeable about every aspect of art. He's incredibly handsome but not conceited about it. He's hardworking and cooperative. He's macho without being a pain in the you-know-what. He admits he's had his heart broken and seems really sensitive."

"Please! Stop!" Barbara raised her hands in mock self-defense. "I can't stand any more of this perfection! Now tell me what's wrong with him."

"What's wrong," Connie answered somberly, "is that he cares more about Art than about his heart. He makes that very clear. And I can't figure out whether I've made any impact on him at all or if I'm just a convenient fling."

"Handy sex, you mean. Umm—" she paused delicately "—does he seem, uh, very experienced?"

"Very. Did I forget to include that in the list of 'perfects?'" Despite herself, she couldn't keep from giggling like a schoolgirl. Bird joined her. It was some time before she noticed that the waiter had reappeared at the table and was waiting politely for their order.

"Oh! Eduardo, forgive us. How are the soft-shell crabs today?"

In an ironic replay of Connie's tête-à-têtes with her clients, the white-jacketed waiter leaned closer to impart a confidence. Concern was written all over his face. "If you will permit me, Mrs. Nathan... I feel I should advise against the crabs. I'm afraid today's delivery was not, shall we say, of the very best quality. May I suggest instead the medallions of lamb? They are perfectly pink and tender, with a rather nice white-wine-and-truffle sauce. And they are served with a bouquet of baby vegetables."

"Sounds good to me. How about you—" she caught herself before "Bird" slipped out "—Barbara?"

"Uh, sure, fine. I'll have the lamb, too."

Writing away smoothly, Eduardo continued his sales pitch. "And may I get you an appetizer? The season's pâté from Dordogne is just in..."

On her own, Connie would have passed by a first course as too much food at lunchtime. But her friend had always been a hearty eater and anyway, she could see Bird was revelling in this haute cuisine fling. "What do you think?" she asked, though the answer was a foregone conclusion. Barbara was nodding vehemently. "You've clinched another deal, Eduardo."

"Grazie, grazie tante, Mrs. Nathan. The wine steward will consult with you shortly."

"Wow, this is living, Fischer, *living!*"

"Yeah, I think I was pretty smart to pick a career category where the boss insists on paying for this, huh? But seriously, this is an important part of the job. I schmooze with those folks out there—" she nodded at the two tables she'd chatted up "—and Villiers, Buck writes it off as a sales expense. But the pressure is still on."

"Dick and I know what that's like, from our experience in Chicago. I almost can feel sorry for you, but..." Bird waved her hands at the luxury surrounding them. The rest of her speech was cancelled due to the appearance of Eduardo bearing two small porcelain plates with the Venezia Azzuro crest in gold and blue. Each plate had a perfect leaf of purple and white radicchio on it and sitting on the leaf was a rich-looking square of pâté plus three tiny *cornichon* pickles no more than two inches in length. "Ooooh," breathed Bird.

"Dig in!" Connie laughed at her friend. "Say, what would you like to do this afternoon?"

"I'd like to get a shotgun and pay a visit to your Mr. Considine and tell him he has to elope with you. But if that's not on the calendar, let's shop!"

And, after their pâté and lamb—followed by the famous dessert wagon, which sent Bird into raptures—shop they did. They walked slowly up Fifth Avenue ogling every window, circling through Saks and Bonwit's and Bergdorf. Then it was across 57th Street to the new international boutique mecca of Madison Avenue. Barbara Hollobird, who'd grown up in the neighborhood, hardly recognized it. "This used to be the shoe repair place," she marveled, gaping at a panoply of antique jewels in the window. "That was the deli—" pointing to an art gallery "—and Old Sal's newsstand was on the corner." This last location was now occupied by a beauty salon that had its own smartly uniformed doorman and a line of limousines waiting out front.

"Amazing, isn't it?" Connie agreed. "Let's cross the street."

"Why?" Bird resisted the tug on her elbow. "I want to check out that handbag shop."

"Because around the corner from the handbag place is the entrance to Kenneth Considine's building. And with my luck, we'll run into him kissing some other woman!"

"Oh, I see." Barbara patted her hand as they cut across the street abruptly. "You've really got it bad." For the next half hour they walked and talked, neither woman seeing the arrays of goods artfully arranged in each window for maximum temptation. They were immersed in Constance's baffling love story, analyzing the possible reasons for Ken's lack of commitment, weighing the chances for triumph or disaster.

By the time Connie snapped to, they had crossed north of 79th Street and were into less rarified air, storewise. "Hey, thanks for listening to me whine. I'll bet your kids would love some souvenirs." She pointed to a shop gaily decorated with balloons, models of the Statue of Liberty and a six-foot, inflatable Godzilla wearing sunglasses.

In a flash, Barbara had taken some of everything and was maneuvering two huge shopping bags out the door. She'd bought I Love New York T-shirts, posters, mugs with each child's name on the side, a blow-up Empire State Building and a sheaf of paper-doll books for her younger daughter. "How am I going to get all this stuff on the plane?" she wondered.

"They'll never let you take it as carry-on," Connie noted expertly, trying to snag a taxi against stiff local competition. When she succeeded, it was a struggle to wedge long-legged Barbara and her bags into the cramped rear seat. "Either get a carton or a real cheap suitcase, pack that stuff in and check it as luggage."

"Good idea." The blonde peered around her purchases. "When will I see you again, Fish?"

"Next time I'm in Florida. That's a promise." Connie bent in for a goodbye hug and peck on the cheek. "Who knows—by then I'll probably be in heaven or hell, emotionally speaking."

"I'll pray hard for the heaven part!" Bird waved through the back window as the cab lurched into congested uptown traffic.

12

IT SEEMED TO CONSTANCE as if things were going faster and faster, time slipping ever more swiftly away. One day—that glorious day!—she and Kenneth Considine had been working in the Vernay library, with almost half the house ahead of them. A blink of the eye and they'd been whipping through the grand salon . . . a second blink and they'd tackled the huge front hall which had so astounded them the day Fitch had unsealed the mansion. Soon, all that would be left would be the dining room, kitchen and pantries.

As Ken had predicted, their love nest was secure. As long as they went inside at 9:00 a.m. and exited promptly at 5:00 p.m., nobody could or would disturb them. Many days, instead of taking a lunch break they made love in the library. Afterward, they would carry sandwiches back to the hall and munch while working. Connie was always careful to sweep up the crumbs.

But no matter what heights that lovemaking took her to, she always crashed to the ground when thoughts came of the day that was marching toward her at a grim pace. That was when the Vernay mansion's front doors would be flung open to the invading armies of the museum and auction house. When the library's contents would be scattered to the four winds. When she and her lover would have to stand, mute, on opposing battle lines for the months it would take to settle the estate completely. They would not dare to meet, to be seen together. How could she possibly stand the absence of his sweet flesh? And would it be difficult for Ken? During that time, would he meet somebody new? Would she, in fact, ever touch him again after they left this house? It was all going too fast!

But not fast enough for Ian Buck. Shrewd and demanding, he noticed that the pace of their cataloguing had slowed down, however infinitesimally. "Let me remind you that we are holding late October and early November open for the Vernay sales. We settled on this schedule, based on the time it took you to complete the upper stories. I do not understand why you're not making swifter progress."

Connie had expected this, and had her story prepared. "Two reasons, Mr. Buck," she replied, her voice as steady as possible. "One is that the bulk of the Marquise's paintings are on the ground floor. We are having considerable differences about their provenance and the comparison with the New York's current inventory. Let me assure you that I am waging vigorous battles for every one, especially the Impressionists. Mr. Considine and I are having some, uh, heated discussions." *What a lie, Constance!*

"I see." The British voice sounded a bit less icy.

"And secondly, we are working on the porcelains and having a devil of a time assembling the sets. We find

Sèvres pieces in the middle of a stack of Chinese export tableware and Meissen mixed in with Imari." That part was certainly true; no sooner would she and Ken laboriously put together and wash several hundred matching dishes—then list and photograph them—than they would come upon another piece of the same pattern. The only solution was to rip out the catalogue page and make a new entry.

"Ah." Her boss had warmed up—a little. "And I suppose the cleaning is arduous as well."

"You're so right, sir. But I understand the pressure of time and am doing my best to speed things along." Which was pretty accurate, except for those golden hours in the library when they lay down on the bed of rugs. Sometimes Ken carried her there, light as a feather in his arms....

THE NEXT DAY, she told him about the conversation with Ian Buck. "Wow, that guy sure keeps the screws on," he said grimly.

"Well, haven't *you* gotten any pressure about finishing this job? Didn't the Museum announce a show date?"

"Sure, but Emilio's just kidding himself." Ken laughed at the thought of the director. "He's never stuck to a schedule in his life. He's got two secretaries and one of them does nothing but follow him around with the appointment calendar. Even so, he's usually about six months late."

"Sounds charming," Connie said wistfully. "We have to log our schedules into the computer so Mr. Buck knows where we are at all times. Last November, I called in and found out he'd cancelled my vacation. Damn!"

"What is it?"

"Another piece of the Fitzhugh gilt. Whose coat of arms is that?" She pointed to the middle of the gold-leafed platter at an armorial device.

Ken groaned and went to the stack of catalogues that kept rising as they moved through the house. "Is there a boar's head on the upper left quarter?"

"Nope. It's a stag."

He groaned again. "Augustine, you're driving me nuts! That platter goes with the MacNair set."

She peered over his shoulder at the page entry and photo. "In the salon—I remember, we put it on the Sheraton console near the fireplace. When we finish this—" Connie nodded at six stunning, golden Venetian candelabra "—I guess we'd better go back and reshoot it before we forget." She resisted a strong urge to kiss the back of his neck.

"I guess." He turned back to the camera and there was silence for several moments. "Listen, Con, I'd hate to think that our, uh, diversions were making trouble for you professionally."

Panic rose suddenly in her throat. "What do you mean?"

He lifted his head from the viewfinder to meet her gaze. "I mean the time we are . . . wasting there, in the library."

Was this how he would end it—break off the affair so nothing would slow down their professional duties? *Make light of it!* she screamed silently at herself. "You call that 'wasting time?'"

Thank God, he was grinning. "No, that's not what I'd call it. But it's sure what your Mr. Buck would call it."

Change the subject. "Not to worry. He always wants everything done faster and cheaper. But you could help me with something."

"Sure. What?"

"Well, I've been giving him a report every day but I haven't kept an *exact* record. Mr. Buck wants a specific tally—the number of items that'll be for sale. Plus an estimate of what percentage of the total house contents is coming to us." She meant Villiers, Buck.

"No problem. I'll run the master list through the computer tonight." One more click of the shutter and they went back to the salon to rerecord the annoying MacNair china set for the third time. Connie's heart was still pounding from the brush with emotional disaster.

What am I more afraid of? she would ask herself from time to time. *Losing my job or losing this man?* When she was home with her son, cooking a meal or reading a bedtime story, the weight of evidence seemed to be with the job. After all, the salary she got from Ian Buck paid for Jeremy's school and his toys and the braces he'd probably need in a few years and the college he would want to attend. She, Connie, did not have to scrimp as many divorced women did, or worry about her ex-husband sending the child-support check on time. Or fight about money with Bob. As long as she could keep the job, their son could have whatever he wanted or needed, and she wouldn't have to deprive herself, either. Really, being a vice president of Villiers, Buck *was* the most important thing.

But every morning Monday through Friday, when she spied Kenneth Considine at the mansion's gate on Sutton Circle, Constance knew she would cheerfully live in a hovel and exist on food stamps if she could do it with him.

AT LEAST SHE HAD GOOD NEWS for her boss. "To tell the truth, sir, I wasn't aware of *quite* how well we've been doing. But here it is in black and white and Mr. Considine himself prepared the figures. Of the total household contents so far, forty-three percent—" she drew a breath to build suspense "—is assigned to the New York Museum of Art."

"Bravo, Constance, bravo!" There was more excitement in his voice than she had ever heard before. "Fifty-seven percent of the Vernay Collection is almost more than one had hoped. And when should our staff be prepared to begin the moving process?"

Another breath, this time in pain. The front hall was almost completed. Dining room, kitchen and pantries could take no more than a month. "Four more weeks, I think."

"That would be, ah..." she could hear the pages of his appointment book flipping "... the third week of August. Good. I shall have everyone ready to begin the transfer on the twenty-third. Good night, Constance." The phone connection was broken; to her, it sounded like a guillotine's blade descending.

13

"JEREMY, YOUR FATHER'S HERE!" she called down the hall, noting on another level that her ex-husband's hairline had staged a retreat.

Piled in the apartment foyer was the paraphernalia necessary for a seven-year-old boy to spend two weeks in the country—two *huge* suitcases which Connie had only been able to close by kneeling on them, plus a zip-up duffel that bulged in odd places because it contained such requisites as a hockey stick and several computer games.

Jeremy appeared in the doorway of his room, but not as she would have liked him to look—he was in tears. "I can't find my glove!" he bawled at the two dismayed adults.

"Sorry," Connie muttered to Bob Nathan. "We've been trying to find that damn baseball glove for two days." Louder, to her son, "I'm afraid you left it at school, dear, and somebody else has it now."

"No, it's here! I know it! Hi, Dad." But he was not budging.

"Hello, son. Can you hurry up, please? Sandy's waiting in the car downstairs." Bob's new wife came complete with an old, spacious farmhouse up in the Hudson River Valley. A great place for a little city kid to spend a couple of weeks' summer vacation with his father, they all agreed. If they could just get him out the door.

"Honey, I'll bet your daddy will be happy to get you a new glove for you to play with in the country."

"I sure will," Bob agreed almost enthusiastically. She knew why he was in such a hurry to be off; despite the fact that double and even triple-parking were a way of life in Manhattan, her ex-husband was perpetually convinced that his car was going to be towed away by the police. "Hey, Con, can you give a hand with this stuff?" He gestured at the luggage. "I'm having trouble with my back again."

"Sure, sure." Her mind, unbidden, made the comparison. Kenneth Considine would have hefted the load easily and held the door for her, to boot. "Let me just go get the keys. Are you ready now, J?"

"Uh-huh." The prospect of a new glove had cleared the emotional storm—and his cute little face—as if by magic. "Dad, Dad, can I play with *cows* when we get to the farm?"

Connie toted the suitcases, Bob dragged the duffel behind him gingerly and Jeremy brought up the rear clutching several last-minute must-haves. As this procession straggled out the front door, Sandy—who was small, freckled and perky—leaped to help. "Oh, Gee, Connie, let me take that. I should have thought . . . you know, Bob's bad back and all."

"No problem." Connie swung the suitcases into the rear of the station wagon as Sandy held it open. "Sorry there's so much stuff, but I didn't want you to have to do a laundry. This should hold him for two weeks."

Sandy, who had no children, obviously hadn't considered the washday implications of young boys. "Oh, I see." She nodded dubiously.

Connie took the duffel from Bob and slung it in, too. "Yeah, he goes through two or three outfits a day." She turned to her son. "Now Jeremy, I want you to be a good boy and do what Daddy and Sandy say and have a wonderful time. Give us a kiss."

In her fond Mommy's heart, she had secretly expected the little boy to be unhappy at parting from her for the first time in his life. A few tears and a lingering hug, perhaps? Wrong! "Am I really going to see *cows*?" was all he said as she put her arms around him. But he did wave goodbye as the car pulled away.

"His first time away from home?" the doorman asked sympathetically as Connie waved back.

"Yes, José. And what a trauma for his mother. But this is my chance to get the apartment cleaner than it's been in years."

Actually, when Bob had called to suggest Jeremy's holiday, she'd immediately had much, much wilder plans. For these few days when she would truly be a single woman again, why not invite Ken over—cook him dinner—maybe even ask him to stay the night? As the end of their time in the Vernay mansion loomed, how very precious that stolen visit might be!

But the scheme crumbled into dust one morning in the house elevator. Dennis Morton was with her; he had stopped by to deliver computer printouts that separated the Vernay Collection—what was known of it so far—into categories for auction purposes. Connie was reading them as the elevator doors opened. "A full week for the jewelry, another one for paintings—when do we sell the *furniture*?" she asked Dennis, and smiled at the woman who was already in the car.

She'd seen this woman several times before—tweedy-looking and nice, with strands of silver in her hair and a harried expression. The reason for that was obvious as she was always carrying fabric swatches or wallpaper samples. One had to smile in sympathy; the newcomer was experiencing the pure agony of remodelling her apartment.

This particular day the tweedy woman smiled back and said, "You're Constance Nathan, aren't you?" The accent was elegant, clipped, upper-class England.

"Why, yes..."

"I saw your picture in *Gotham Magazine* and Ian has been saying such wonderful things about you."

Connie drew a blank. "Ian?"

"Oh, do forgive me. Ian Buck. He and my husband were at Eton together and he's been ever so kind since Clive—that's my husband—accepted a fellowship at Columbia University."

As the elevator descended to the lobby Constance introduced her assistant and they went through the polite ritual. "Welcome to the building, if I can be of any help... We were supposed to move in two weeks ago but the plumbers haven't finished.... I hope things go more smoothly and you enjoy your new home."

Dennis was strangely silent until they were in a cab. "Whew! That was close!"

"What?"

"I was just about to say that Mr. Buck was driving us all nuts with his crazy scheduling—when that woman opened her mouth! The guy has spies everywhere!" Dennis got out at Park Avenue and they were almost at Sutton Place when it hit Connie; she could never invite Kenneth Considine to her home until the Vernay estate was settled. Otherwise, that kindly looking woman could destroy her with a chance meeting and a few heedless words in her employer's ear.

So now here it was, the second Saturday in August, and neither son nor lover was available. Work had proceeded on schedule; only a corner of the kitchen and one pantry lay ahead. Which meant that *Thursday* the army of movers would charge the mansion and the beautiful times in the library would be no more. And Kenneth Considine had still not uttered a single word about what would come after that.

Grimly, she set about cleaning the apartment from one end to the other. Starting with the kitchen. *First, get rid of all those spoiling odds and ends in the fridge. On the third shelf, behind the half-head of cabbage, what's that?*

It was Jeremy's baseball glove. His mother laughed so hard she collapsed onto the linoleum.

KEN LAUGHED, TOO, when she told him the story on Monday. "Careful with that tureen!" Connie warned. It was a rare treasure—a covered Imari bowl, glowing with intense blue and copper enamels.

"But why in the refrigerator?"

"I figure he came home from the park after playing baseball, and decided to bend the rules a little and sneak a soda. Then maybe he heard me coming, made a quick getaway and forgot the glove. But what gets me is, I called last night and he didn't seem to care about it at all—after making that big fuss. Uh, how many lots do you think we should make of this Imari?"

"Good question. I see three different underglazes," Ken said, pointing out minute differences in color and refraction, "and dates of manufacture—oh, say thirty to fifty years apart. Ordinarily, I'd just classify Imari by the condition it's in—"

The front-door chimes rang, interrupting his professorial lecture. "Ah, Fitch summons us." He brushed a lock of dark hair out of his eyes.

"We're a little ahead of schedule anyway," Connie noted as they dutifully picked up their possessions and got ready to leave.

"I know." He was smiling mischievously—and sensually. "I think we should plan to . . . celebrate on Wednesday." The meaning couldn't be clearer; they kissed quickly before he opened the big front door. She hoped she wasn't blushing too obviously.

WEDNESDAY MORNING the team arrived with unusual luggage. Ken was toting a big styrofoam cooler of the type associated with beer, football games and tailgate parties. But it held two bottles of Moët et Chandon champagne on ice—"So we can wind this up in style," he announced to everyone concerned.

Connie had racked her brain for gift ideas; what would Fitch and the other two regular guards like? Couldn't be anything too valuable or it would smack of a bribe: Fitch the Scrupulous would be offended. And it should be something that would always remind them of this unusual job they'd performed so well. Not so much as a pin had vanished from her home since the Marquise de Vernay had died.

Inspiration struck while she was passing a trophy shop on Eighth Avenue. Commemorative mugs! On the spot she ordered three silver tankards, each to be engraved with an image of the mansion. Below that, To Alfred Fitch, To Bob Lincoln and To Ramon Acevedo For Performance Above and Beyond the Call of Duty, The Vernay Mansion, New York City, and the dates of their stewardship.

On the front steps that last morning, Connie and Ken formally thanked "the other half of the team." She was glad to see that the mugs struck just the right note with the guards. Ken uncorked one of the jeroboams with a flourish and even Fitch didn't decline the champagne.

The other bottle went inside with the two of them—where they had 'just a few more things to clean up'—straight to the library, where they spent practically the whole day making love. Connie had never been so happy, or so miserable. Never had a man's body and mind satisfied her as Kenneth Considine's did. Never had the prospect of parting caused such pain. Even as he was on top of her and in her, between waves of physical pleasure, she ached to ask "What will happen to us?" Tears flowed from her eyes even as she moaned in ecstasy. He kissed them away and she pulled him even closer, even deeper, each hand clasping a slim, muscular buttock.

Four-thirty found them sitting together on the bed of rugs, sipping champagne from paper cups.

"When is Villiers, Buck holding the sales?" It was the first word he'd said about the future. And he sounded grim; of course, he was bidding farewell to the bulk of the Vernay Collection.

"Second week in October through first week in November." It was going to be a terrific task to get everything moved, listed and displayed in less than two months. But Ian Buck was marshaling every single resource at his command. He was determined that the Vernay auctions would take place during the height of New York's social season, when the cream of international society and money would be in town. "I'll see you then?"

"Hey, Connie, we'll both be here tomorrow, and for however long it takes to clear this place out."

"Won't be the same," she answered somberly. He nodded agreement and was stroking her cheek lightly when the peal of the doorbell ended their idyll.

14

IAN BUCK OBEYED the photographer's instruction, but without enthusiasm. "If you and Mr. Sant'Angelo could just shake hands?" the man called out. He fiddled with the camera that was pointed at the front door of the Vernay mansion. A few people from the apartment house across Sutton Circle stopped to rubberneck but it was hard to see anything past the army of movers and fleets of trucks and cars wedged into the cul-de-sac.

Somebody in publicity had sent the photographer to record the occasion of the mansion's unsealing. So the movers and curators and appraisers stood on the lawn and waited as their respective leaders made a formal show of friendship. Actually, Connie thought, Emilio Sant'Angelo looked as if he held no grudges—even though the New York had come out with the short end of the stick. Ian Buck, however, grasped the museum director's hand as if it were a dead and malodorous fish.

Being very, very careful, Connie had greeted Kenneth Considine with formal gravity and moved away some distance. There was a bit of shock at seeing him in business attire. She'd fallen in love with a man in Levis and those omnipresent cowboy boots. In a tan whipcord suit with tassel loafers, he was almost a stranger.

Guess I *look different too,* she reminded herself. The new lavender linen suit was terrifically flattering and a bone-colored lizard purse-attaché she'd picked up last year was the perfect accessory.

"Fine, fine," The photographer had snapped several shots of Buck and Sant'Angelo; now he was looking about in the crowd. "Could we have the appraising team, too? Mrs. Nathan? Mr. Considine?"

Stiffly, she mounted the steps and stood beside Ian Buck, grinning—not too idiotically, she hoped—for the camera. The flash captured the quartet with Ken on the other end. She could feel Emilio Sant'Angelo's eyes on her, sparkling with lively interest.

"Kenneth, Kenneth!" He rolled the name off his tongue with a rich accent. "Why do you never tell me how lovely, how charming this Mrs. Nathan is? Why all the time you tell me only how tough she is, that she gets all this..." he enquired, waving at the mansion behind them, "for her company?"

Connie laughed nervously. Obviously her lover had played the same game of masquerades she had—tell the boss how disagreeable your partner is, how much the two of you are fighting, to throw up a smokescreen.

"Thank you, Mr. Buck, Mr. Sant'Angelo. Now let's just have the team that went in there and did the job."

Even more stiffly, she shook his hand. Thank God, Ken kept a straight face. Only somebody as near as she was could see the twinkle in his blue eyes. Her own expression was blank, she was pretty sure.

As their watch neared its end, Fitch and his men were obviously taking no last-minute chances on security. Extra guards were everywhere, and Fitch himself was at the door to check credentials before anyone entered. But the crowd was excited and, as he worked keys in the locks, it pressed closer. In the crush a skinny, bespectacled man from the New York accidentally stepped on the tail of Fitch's dog.

Perfectly trained, the German shepherd didn't make a sound—he just jumped on his tormentor. By the time his master turned around, the dog was standing on the skinny man's chest, looking deep into terrified eyes and awaiting command.

"Off, Victor, off!" Fitch said firmly. Connie could tell he was trying hard not to laugh. Victor obediently removed his front paws from the prone executive and sat down, tongue lolling. As he helped the man up and dusted him off, the guard raised his voice. "Now, folks, if you'll just relax. It'll be a few more minutes before anything can be removed."

True. The heads of the museum and auction house had requested an exclusive, preview tour of the mansion before it was stripped of its riches. Fitch ceremoniously held the door as the Briton and the Italian swept in.

"Careful, gentlemen!" Connie warned as she followed. "It's sort of a rabbit warren in there."

There was a small crash and a stream of fluid Latin curses. Emilio Sant'Angelo was clutching his forehead. "No, no! Was my fault, I was looking at the tapestry." He waved away attempts at help.

The small parade went single file through the house with Ken leading and Connie gritting her teeth every step of the way. The museum director expostulated steadily, often in his native tongue, over the treasures. "Ma'—it's gorrrgeous!" he trilled at a Venetian landscape painting. "What perfection!" he said, saluting a suite of Russian rosewood furniture inlaid with ivory—which was allotted for sale.

Ian Buck said nothing. He was busy writing in a leather notebook. Connie knew he was deciding which items should be pitched to which customers, and what sales tactics should be employed to maximize profit.

She didn't even dare to glance at her lover until they reached the library, but he was displaying the Van Eyck to his superior and took no notice of her. "Heaven!" Sant'Angelo cried, pressing his hands together as if in prayer.

The tour ended at the safe hidden in the upstairs linen closet. Connie did the honors here. She worked the combination and pulled open the rusty door. The pair of plum leather boxes were on top. Raising the lid, she displayed the splendor of the Petrov diadem.

Even Emilio was silent. As the four of them stared at the tiara's sparkling perfection, she realized ruefully that each was seeing something different. Ken saw a terrible loss to the museum and community at large. His boss saw beauty and dazzling artistry. She, herself, was remembering the painful day the diadem was discovered—and the glorious times that followed. And Ian Buck? She was pretty sure he was thinking how to hype the bidding for it.

The quartet wound their careful way back to the front hall where Fitch still held off the hordes. Seeing them, the crowd surged forward again. "We can't let all these people in here," Ken cautioned. "Things will be damaged."

"Yes," Ian Buck agreed. He extended a long, bony hand and beckoned two men wearing the brown-and-gold uniform of his company. "Just you two to begin with." It was a command.

Behind him, the museum director erupted. "So! *Your* people are to get in here before *my* people?" he screamed, turning quite red in the face. "You think this is *your* house, perhaps?"

Ian Buck was taken aback by Emilio's fury. "Really, it was just a suggestion to get started. If you insist . . ." He let the sentence trail away.

With great vigor and a grand gesture, Sant'Angelo signaled to a man and woman wearing the colors of the New York—navy and powder blue.

It was rather like an antique, ceremonial dance, Connie mused. A gavotte, wasn't that the word? The two pairs of movers advanced into the hall with measured step. She pointed to a pair of malachite tables—Russian, early 19th cent. prob. origin, Winter Palace, St. Petersburg—that stood near the door. The brown-and-gold team gingerly picked them up. Ken indicated the set of gold Venetian candelabra. "They're heavy," he warned the team, "one at a time." The blue-clad pair extended gloved hands and wrapped them around the bases of two pieces. Then the four movers retreated in lockstep.

Outside, the assemblage oohed and aahed at the first sight of the Vernay Collection.

The gavotte continued in silence for a while until the museum director's natural ebullience overcame him again. "So much beauty in such a small space—I'm growing faint. I need coffee." He looked hopefully at Kenneth Considine.

"Sorry, Emilio. Nothing in the kitchen works."

"He's right, Signor Sant'Angelo," Connie chimed in. "The refrigerator was broken by the time we got here. And we had the gas line shut down for fear of fire. It was leaking in several places."

The Italian was horrified. "But—you have been working in conditions of great hardship!"

"It was a privilege," she said with a smile. "Just to see all this." She waved at the grand array of items that surrounded them and filled the house.

"Ah yes, yes." Sant'Angelo bobbed a little courtly bow, his eyes flickering shrewdly between her and—*Good God! He's made the connection!* her instincts yelled. *Keep your face absolutely blank, you fool!*

The terror of the moment slipped away as the Director straightened his jacket and brushed some dust off its silk shoulders. "Regrettably, I am being of no help here and must get back to my office. Signora—" he bowed to Connie again "—gentlemen—" a decidedly cold bow to Ian Buck and a slap on the shoulder for Kenneth Considine "—I bid you good day." Emilio Sant'Angelo swept out the door to his waiting limousine, pulling several underlings along in his wake.

"Hmm." Buck was finally closing his little notebook and slipping the carnelian fountain pen into a pocket. "I see that my usefulness here is also limited. Constance, I would appreciate a status report tonight. Mr. Considine . . ." The thought was not completed aloud but anyone could fill in the blanks: Mr. Considine, watch yourself and no tricks with *my* Vernay Collection.

"Goodbye, sir."

Ken said nothing until her boss was also in his car and it was pulling away. "What a cold bastard." He shook himself as if trying to shed a wet cloak.

Connie looked around the circle of space that was now clear. "I guess the rest of them—" she meant the movers waiting outside "—could start now, huh?" She waved from the doorway to Dennis Morton and the crowd stirred into action. Her assistant was in charge of the Villiers, Buck movers; he carried a massive clipboard and wore a serious expression to go with his navy pinstripe suit. "You, too!" she shouted to the young woman heading the Museum phalanx. With a drum-majorette gesture the girl dispatched her troops.

Uniformed teams advanced briskly on the house. "Here comes the army of worker ants," Connie muttered to Ken, glad to see his responsive grin. It was an apt metaphor. In minutes the Marquise's home was a giant anthill bustling with energetic toilers.

By midafternoon the front hall was completely bare; Fitch's footsteps echoed on the flagstones. "Mrs. Nathan?" he called.

"In here!" she yelled back from the salon, which was being dismantled with appalling speed.

"Ma'am, there is a call for you—a phone in the car."

"For me? Who is it?"

"Mr. Menlow from Cutting, Menlow and Wilmot. Several members of the Carmody family are in his office, he says."

"Okay, Fitch, thanks."

"What's that about?" Ken asked. He was helping two men from the New York extract a delicate gilded chaise longue—early 19th cent., French Empire, poss. property of Empress Josephine at Malmaison—from a tangled mass of furniture.

"Oh, the Carmodys have been bugging us for a dollar figure. Mr. Buck told them he refuses to guess what the sale will bring until we do the publicity stuff. So now they're probably trying me. It's a good thing nobody had a car phone parked outside before this. We'd have never finished."

"Right," he grinned slyly. The smile clearly meant "Or done some other things."

The call was as she predicted. Dennis was in the rear seat of a Villiers, Buck limousine; as she joined him he clicked the speakerphone. A man was yelling ". . . and

I'm sick and tired of this crap!" behind the suave tones of Morgan Menlow III.

"Ah, Mrs. Nathan, thank you for tearing yourself away from your work. As you can understand, my clients—the Carmody family, that is—have been waiting quite a while for an accurate estimate of the sale value of their portion of the Vernay estate."

"All we get is excuses!" the same voice yelled. "What we want is a number."

"Yes," Menlow cut in. "We'd appreciate your input in this matter, as someone most familiar with the collection."

Connie cleared her throat. "Well, that depends."

"Depends on *what*?" the yeller responded.

"Mr. Carmody, in a sale like this, each object has two values or price tags, speaking practically. One price is what the thing is worth *intrinsically*—that is, as a work of art of and by itself. The second price is what we can command *historically*—what its reputation and the reputation of its previous owners add to the value in the eyes of its beholders. Am I clear?"

"Sort of." The impatient heir was calming down. "Go on."

"Let's say we have—oh, a painting by Manet, a small landscape, very charming, fully authenticated, unusual. Now, if it is offered for sale anonymously—if we don't specify where the work came from—it might go for three-point-five million dollars on today's market. That's the *intrinsic* price."

The yeller whistled.

"Yes, it's a nice sum. But if the auction house can tell bidders that this Manet has a fascinating provenance—that its owners have been celebrities or nobility—then it will fetch even more. For instance, if we knew that the Manet was once owned by the King of Greece and then by Aly Khan, it might command as much as four and a half to five million. That's because its history gives it cachet."

"So call me stupid," Carmody was blustering again. "We know where my great-aunt's stuff came from, don't we? And how she got it? Why can't anybody give me a number?"

"We have no benchmark," Connie explained patiently. "Your great-aunt the Marquise never sold a thing, so we have no idea what her reputation is worth to the buying public. It may add a lot, as with the Duchess of Windsor's estate. Or it could *hurt* values, as in the Goering auction." As Hitler's right-hand man, *Reichsmarschall* Goering had commandeered art from all over Europe. "Everybody expected his notoriety and expertise would make the sale a smash. But it turned out that private collectors didn't want to touch the stuff. Most of it ended up in museums at bargain prices."

"Oh," said Mr. Carmody.

"Naturally, as part of our sales program, we at Villiers, Buck will be doing our utmost to stimulate interest in the Vernay Collection. I'm sure our publicity department has some very creative plans. Perhaps, once everything is arranged in the galleries, you'd like to talk it over with us?" Which, of course, was what Ian Buck had been saying all along.

"Uh, yeah, sure."

"We appreciate your most helpful chat, Mrs. Nathan." Morgan Menlow III was clearly grateful to have his client defused.

"My pleasure, Mr. Menlow. And I hope we'll see you at the sale." Why not ask? Mr. M. M. The Third was sitting on a pile of old money and his wife had begun to collect *Régence* funiture. "Goodbye."

Crossing the lawn, she noted sadly that the grass was being trampled into oblivion by the army of workers marching to and from their trucks. Quite symbolic, that. Then there was the bare front hall, its grimness and size—and years' worth of dust—made shocking by total nakedness. But wait! The bustling noise of the movers had receded from the salon. They'd finished it off already? That meant, oh no . . .

Across the salon was a door leading to a second, smaller hallway. And across from that, the next logical room to tackle would be the library.

Connie was frozen by the salon's entrance as a pair of "her" movers appeared. "Hi, Mrs. Nathan," they greeted her cheerfully. "Jeez, there sure are a lot of rugs in there."

"Sure are," she responded with difficulty. Her throat was dry and aching and her heart thumped unpleasantly in her chest. Rolled into a neat tube, the carpet they were carrying out was tagged: Indo-Pak/Afghan silk carpet, 12′3″ × 18′6″. Prob. mid-19th cent. Qum.

Without thinking, she fled upstairs and took refuge in Augustine's bedroom, fighting back tears.

Some time later the man who'd lain on the carpet with her found her there, staring out the windows at the eddying waters of the East River. "Connie...there you are. Are you okay?"

"What? Oh, hi Ken. Sure, I'm fine. It just *got* to me down there—know what I mean?"

"Seeing everything torn apart like that." He nodded somberly. "It's really the end of an epoch—the dispersal of one of the greatest collections of all times."

The dispersal that was bothering her was simply the dismantling of their "bed" and the rest of the library—but why be a fool and let him know? Perched on the window seat that lined the curving tower wall, she gazed around for another topic of conversation. Here was where their Herculean labors had begun. "Hey, you know something?" Reflexively she unfolded her legs and headed across the room. "I don't think we ever looked inside this."

"This" was the coffer, which sat off to the side, between the canopied bed and windows. When it was new, in the sixteenth century, it would have been used to store folded clothing. After the idea of hanging garments in a wardrobe became fashionable, these chests were easily converted to hold bed linens and comforters. This particular one stood staunchly and massively on four stubby legs, its elaborate carvings cut directly into heavy walnut, blackened by time. When Connie walked over to it, it was as high as her waist and longer than the spread of her two arms.

She hooked fingers under the lip of the lid and tried to lift. "I guess it's locked."

Ken came over and eyed the heavy oblong with interest. "More likely rusted. Or maybe dry rot," he said firmly, assuming the same stance she'd taken. He yanked with vigor—and results. The lid rose with rending sounds as ancient wood crumbled and old metal gave way. Eddies of dust swirled in the air; Connie fanned her hands to get it out of their faces.

Then she leaned over and looked inside the long-sealed chest. With great difficulty, she stifled a scream.

15

"IT'S A BODY," she whispered frantically. "A skeleton!"

"Two skeletons," Ken corrected.

Her stomach churning, Constance ventured another peek into the chest. He was right; the remains of two human beings rested there. The top one lay facedown on the bottom one in a grisly parody of lovemaking. "Who are they—I mean were they?" she wondered.

"They've been dead a long, long time." Ken sounded calm but his face showed the same shock she felt. "And look, I think they were murdered." He pointed to a hole in the back of the top skull and a similar aperture in the temple of the lower one.

"Shot! Oh, my God!" It came out as a gasp. "Well, whoever did them in may be dead by now, too."

They stared wide-eyed at each other as the implications sank in. As if pulled by a magnet, the pair swiveled to look at the bed of the late Augustine Carmody Cheney d'Urso de Vernay. "Do you suppose..."

Ken nodded grimly. "I do indeed. She could hardly have shared a bedroom with two corpses without knowing about it. But who? And why?"

The bone lizard attaché still held her notebook with the copies of old newspaper stories Dennis had complied. But Connie didn't have to reread them to remember. "I'll bet it's the first husband, Cheney. Everybody thought he skipped town when he vanished, but . . ."

"Good thinking! Didn't you say his girlfriend disappeared at the same time? Maybe Augustine blew them *both* away. But how did she get the bodies in here with nobody knowing?"

Their musings were interrupted by noise from the movers below. "They'll be coming up here soon. What are we going to do?" Staring at the makeshift grave, she panicked. "If we call the cops, they could seal the house up for years. Mr. Buck will kill *me* if this sale doesn't happen on schedule—and what will happen to bidding prices when people find out all this stuff was collected by a murderess?"

Ken chuckled sardonically. "The old girl sure was full of surprises. She must have known we'd find the skeletons and what that would mean."

Connie had an idea. "Couldn't we, uh, 'wait' to find them until the place is cleared out?" she offered hopefully. "Then if they lock the joint up it won't matter." Looking at her lover's face, searching for agreement, she found instead . . . the Man of Principle had reappeared.

And he was looking more than a little disgusted with her proposed chicanery. "I'm not going to break the law for a smart career move." The sarcasm was heavy.

"No, I guess not," she sighed. "Oh, this is going to be awful." Another sigh. "I'll go call the police."

"And I'll tell everybody they have to get out until the investigation is finished," Ken answered. He put a finger under her chin to lift it and dusted her lips with a light kiss. "Hey, Connie, everything's okay as long as you know you're doing the right thing."

The touch and the tenderness were enough to keep her going through the rest of it, even when she phoned Ian Buck. He asked exactly what she dreaded. "Why didn't you keep this quiet until the estate was dispersed?"

"I thought of that, sir, but Mr. Considine refused."

"You've told me he's a difficult man." Buck bit off the words with acidity. "You didn't tell me he's an obstinate fool." What could she say in response? Silence was the best course, though the sound of her boss blowing air through his teeth was ominous, a sure indication of rage. "Let me know what happens when the police arrive. If they make any serious trouble, call immediately. I have a valuable contact at City Hall. And now I'll have to talk with our attorneys." The phone was slammed down with a crash. Connie winced.

"I'm in trouble," she told Ken, who joined her in the Villiers, Buck limo after shooing everyone out of the mansion. "He came very close to firing me on the spot, and believe me, I've seen it happen. It's my job to get the Vernay Collection on the market, period, no matter what it takes."

"That's ridiculous!" Ken exploded. "Doesn't the man think of anything but the bottom line?"

"Nope," she said flatly. "Your turn," she added, pointing to the phone.

He lifted the handset and punched buttons. "Emilio, are you sitting down? Good. Because we found two skeletons in the Vernay Mansion and we've had to call in the police." The phone squealed in horror. "No, they were dead a long time. The worst part is, we think the Marquise killed them. And that it was her first husband and his mistress." The phone made noises of comprehension; after all, the crime of passion was a Latin invention. "What we're afraid of is that they'll seal the mansion pending a criminal investigation . . . No, I have no idea how long it could be. Oh, here they come now."

That much was obvious from the rising din of sirens. A flotilla of blue-and-white cars, lights flashing, wedged itself among the trucks at the end of Sutton Circle. "I'll call you as soon as I know anything more." Ken hung up.

"He's not mad at you?" Connie asked in disbelief.

There was no time to answer. The limousine door was abruptly opened by a policeman. "You the two that found the bodies?" he asked.

16

LIEUTENANT MCHUGH SURVEYED the tower bedroom glumly. "You didn't touch anything, I hope."

"We touched *everything,*" Connie said truthfully.

"We've been working in here for six months," Ken explained.

"And you didn't happen to notice two bodies that were lying around?"

Ken cleared his throat nervously. "Well, Lieutenant, the truth is we forgot to open the chest until today."

"It's not as if they were smelling or anything." The words were out before she thought; she was rewarded with a skeptical and disapproving look from the policeman.

"Aw, gimme a break!" she added peevishly.

"Local girl," McHugh grunted. "You're so smart, tell me who they were."

"As a matter of fact—" she brandished her notebook and opened it to an old news photo of Harry Cheney "—as a matter of fact, we think it was this guy. Her first husband—the Marquise de Vernay's, that is."

"Yeah?" McHugh took the notebook. "Financier Vanishes," he read aloud. "Mr. Cheney Last Seen At Wall Street Office. Heiress Wife Distraught. Huh. So who's the second body?"

Connie flipped to another page, an article written some twenty years later. Unsolved Manhattan Mysteries was the headline. She jabbed a finger at the line she wanted McHugh to read.

"Cheney Disappearance, 1924. Social Register stockbroker vanishes with blond speakeasy dancer and seventeen million dollars of his wife's money." The cop whistled and looked inside the chest again. And read some more while Connie, Ken and several other policemen stood quietly in the oppressive room. "Very slick." He closed the notebook and handed it to its owner—then turned to Augustine's massive bed.

"Did you disturb anything? What are these books doing here?"

"Folios," Ken corrected. "Quite valuable, fine art."

"We took them off the bed to photograph on top of the chest," Connie chimed in. "Then we put them back."

"She slept with books?" McHugh seemed baffled. "A weirdo. Gimme a hand." Dutifully, the bystanders helped him move the folios from bed to window seat. The detective peered intently at the moldy comforter, then pulled it and the sheets below it off the bed.

Here was another antique, but not the valuable kind. It was a mattress, mottled brown and green with age; springs poked through in several places and sprigs of horsehair protruded. The mattress cover had once been satin and its elaborate brocade patterning could still be discerned in places.

But what McHugh did was even odder; he pointed the forefinger of each hand like a gun barrel and plunged them into the mattress. They seemed to go in easily. "Pow," he said softly. "Pow." Sticking his thumbs into the holes as well, he extracted two small rusty objects. Bullets.

"Ah." Kenneth Considine breathed a sound of enlightenment. "She didn't have to bring the bodies here. They *were* here."

Connie stared at him and at the policeman. "You mean they—Cheney and his girlfriend—were in Augustine's bed?" she asked incredulously. For some strange, perverse reason she was feeling feminine outrage on behalf of the late Marquise—who was, after all, a murderess.

At the lieutenant's direction, a police photographer entered and recorded everything—the chest with skeletons; the bullet-riddled mattress, with white tape inserted to show the angle of penetration; the bullets themselves. The harsh glare of strobe lights made the scene even more surreal. Then came forensics—two scholarly-looking men who muttered over the chest and took measurements and notes. During this quiet time Constance decided to make her appeal.

"Excuse me, Lieutenant, but what happens now?"

"Next thing is we take the skeletons and the chest and the mattress to the lab. Not that we're gonna find out anything conclusive. They didn't even have dental charts in those days, so we may never establish identity. But my guess is, you're right about this. So then we take statements from you two and close the books."

"That's it? That's all?" Hope was beginning to rise in her chest.

McHugh was patient, almost patronizingly so. "Lady, even a suspicious guy like me doesn't think *you* could've killed two people and magically aged the corpses by sixty years. Even if what's-her-name—"

"The Marquise de Vernay," Connie supplied helpfully.

"Yeah, even if she didn't do it—and it sure looks like she did—whoever the killer was is gone by now. And we've got hotter murder cases than this to work on—much hotter."

"So, uh, your guys cart the evidence away and we can go back to work here?"

He gave her the shrewd policeman's eyes again. "Yeah, unless you want us to seal the place up and search for more clues or something."

Connie clutched his arm in supplication. "No! That's exactly what I don't want! I've got to get this stuff to the auction gallery in the next week. It's my job we're talking about here, McHugh."

The streetwise policeman could see right through her, she felt. He was judging—is this woman honest? Is she hiding something? But she passed the test; he patted her hand in a kindly manner. "So, get back to work" was all he said.

"Thanks a million!" In the headlong rush to reach the car phone and give her boss the good news, she paused only to mutter "He says we can go ahead," to Ken.

He was right on her heels as they reached the vestibule. The young policeman standing by the door said laconically, "Watch out—the circus has come to town."

His meaning became clear when the door opened. Now, in addition to the moving vans and their crews and the police cars and ambulances—rather too late for that, Connie thought—there was a squadron of shiny panel trucks with slogans painted on the sides and strange dishlike contraptions attached to the roofs. As she and Ken emerged, these trucks turned on glaring lights aimed right at their faces. Through the fence, arms stuck out microphones in their direction.

The voices behind the arms knew their names. "Mrs. Nathan, over here!" one commanded. "Channel Three Eyewitness News, Ken," another called familiarly.

"Tell us about the bodies."

"Who were they?"

"Is it true she hid them under the bed?"

"Why did you cover this up so long, Mrs. Nathan?"

The accusation stung her into reply. "There's been no cover-up. They were found today in a locked chest that had to be forced open."

"Good, good," Ken whispered. Raising his voice, he added, "Lieutenant McHugh is investigating and he'll tell you everything you need to know."

But that didn't satisfy the news-hungry pack. As the two of them fought their way to the limousine they were battered by questions, demands, pleas and threats. By the time they reached sanctuary, the barrage had extracted most of what Connie and Ken knew. And, presumably, sent it out over the airwaves.

As the long, sleek car pulled out of Sutton Circle, she phoned Ian Buck at home. "I just saw you on the television," he said, pronouncing it "tellyvision." She could read nothing from his tone of voice.

"Mr. Buck, the police have given permission for us to proceed with emptying the house."

There was a pause, then, tentatively, "Really?"

"Yes, sir. I made a personal appeal to the officer in charge and he agreed it's an open-and-shut case. The only thing that's impounded is the chest the, uh, remains were in. And the mattress—Augustine apparently surprised them in her *own* bed."

"So I gather. Well—" warmth had returned to the clipped, dry voice "—well, this is splendid news, indeed. I must admit I suspected your judgment in notifying these annoying authorities before the job is done. But you do seem to have carried it off, Constance. And some sort of notoriety couldn't be avoided."

She was breathing easier, much easier, but there were still pitfalls ahead. "We can only hope, sir, that this discovery does not damage the reputation of the Vernay Collection."

"Ah, yes. Confidentially, my dear, I rather think the opposite will be true. Nothing like a juicy little scandal to bring out the best in our clientele. Let me know how you proceed tomorrow."

Connie sighed with relief as the connection was broken. "Looks like those paychecks will keep on coming." Ken noted sardonically.

"Don't even joke about it," she said sotto voce. The driver was, after all, on Ian Buck's payroll, too. For his benefit she added loudly, "Would you like to call Signor Sant'Angelo now?"

"No, thanks. Emilio will want all the salacious details and I'll be on the phone for hours. It'll wait."

It was then Constance realized Kenneth had inserted his left hand under her bottom and was squeezing her right buttock most provocatively. With the driver there, ears alert and eyes on the rearview mirror, there was nothing she could do to stop it. Not that she wanted to.

17

As a mother, Constance had many opportunities to observe the behavior of children in toy stores. Most kids went into a state she called 'toy lust'—they became hyperactive and tore around the premises crying "I want it! I want it!" at everything—until the prospect of imminent bankruptcy forced Mommy or Daddy to collar and tow them away. But some children were subject to 'toy coma,' so dazzled by the splendors before them that they became catatonic and unable to move.

For better or worse, Jeremy Nathan was a 'toy-coma' boy. Even a small assortment would hynotize him utterly. So his mother had carefully avoided exposing him to F.A.O. Schwarz, New York's biggest, most posh emporium for children. When Jeremy was invited to a birthday party for Brian Herman—who still had no front teeth and was the class Spitting Champion, as her son had informed her—ugh!—her plan was a solo gift-buying visit to Schwarz. Maybe during lunch hour, or right after work.

But there had simply been no time for it. The month and a half since the Vernay mansion was emptied had been the most exhausting of her professional life. As the riches filled the galleries and workshops of Villiers,

Buck, an army of cleaners, conservators, restorers and appraisers descended upon them.

And that army personally reported to her, Constance Nathan with an unceasing chorus of questions, requests and disputes. Why had she described this armoire as late eighteenth century when it could be *early* and thus more valuable? Where was the third Medici portrait described in Volume II of the catalogue, page 346? It was on the reverse side of the fourth portrait, she explained patiently, concealed within the frame. And what was she going to do about Neville, "who is pretending to be an authority on Austro-Hungarian crystal when he actually knows less about it than my dog does?"

The demands followed her out of the office and into her home. Dinners were often interrupted by phone calls and messengers bearing documents marked *Urgent!* Sometimes she invited Dennis Morton to join them just so they could catch up on paperwork after Jeremy's bedtime. Fast food and restaurant deliveries became staples and household cleaning a catch-as-catch-can affair. At the end of each marathon day, she would crawl into her own bed, bone-tired.

Only then did she have the chance to think about Kenneth Considine—and to ache for his touch and presence. To wait for his phone call, or call him herself. To brood about the reasons why he never, ever referred to any future for them, no matter how fond he seemed. On the one hand, she impatiently counted the days until the Vernay storm would have passed and she could see him again. The other side of her mind was profoundly terrified. Maybe he was trying to tell her they had *no* future?

Ken was as busy as she, with his own army of artisans and laborers toiling at top speed to meet a show deadline. "And I actually think we're on schedule," he said with a laugh. But even if there had been time for a rendezvous, notoriety would have made it risky. That August night at the Vernay mansion, with the glare of television lights blinding them, was just the beginning of a media blitz.

The tabloids took up the cry. Marquise Shot Hubby and Blonde In Own Bed! screamed the *Post*, Hid Crime in Chest for Sixty Years. *People* magazine ran a comprehensive cover feature on the late Augustine de Vernay, including the appealing photo of her as a young girl that had first intrigued Constance. Reporters lurked outside the auction house on Park Avenue and the museum uptown, hoping for more tidbits, more scandal. "Didn't I see you on TV?" asked the salesgirl when Connie bought moisturizer. "Here's the celebrity!" joked the deli counterman as he made her a Reuben sandwich.

After a while, Kenneth Considine simply refused to spend time on any more interviews. But she couldn't. "No, no Constance!" scolded Ian Buck when she was invited for a *City Live* news segment on Channel Three. "You mustn't decline. I understand you have many demands on your time, but this exposure is invaluable. The whole Vernay affair is fascinating—I'm asked about it wherever I go. There is simply no way we could buy this kind of publicity. And you do it so well."

He was really laying it on thick and she knew why. Ian Buck made a poor spokesman for his own company. On television, he came across as quite unpleasant; Connie had seen a videotape once, before it was quickly destroyed. "Oh, by the by, Lady FitzGibbon was saying how charming she finds you."

Who? "Beg your pardon . . ."

"Delia FitzGibbon. She and Lord FitzGibbon have taken a flat in your building."

Aha—the nice, tweedy British woman on the elevator—and her husband had a title. Which explained why Ian Buck was friendly with a mere college professor. And reminded her yet again that there was no way "that Considine fellow" could visit. The thought which tormented her most was that Ken could be seeing any other woman in New York with no trouble at all.

"Let me know when the *City Live* interview will run," Buck concluded. "And there's a critic from the *Times* who wants to talk to you. I gave her your number."

Jeremy was almost as tired of the brouhaha as his mother. "I saw your Mom on TV" had gotten to be an old hat line at the playground. He made it clear that Mom-at-home-by-six-with-dinner-ready was more to his liking than Mother the Celebrity. Guiltily, Connie promised to devote maximum time to her son when this job was finished. Of course, Jeremy asked every day when that would be.

The pressure ground on her steadily as September dwindled toward October. And then there was the birthday party for Brian Herman. All week, she tried to squeeze in a half hour or so to pop over to F.A.O. Schwarz and pick up something appropriate—but never got out of the office until the toy store was long closed. Saturday, the day of the party, found mother and son headed out early to shop. Connie allowed an hour and a half.

As expected, Jeremy got the worst case of 'toy coma' she'd ever seen. Simply approaching the building on Fifth Avenue—its glass walls revealing the three stories of riches inside—made his step slow, and he dragged on her hand. The centerpiece of the ground floor was a giant animated clock trimmed with moving wooden soldiers, flying fairies and a galloping giraffe; the boy's mouth fell open and stayed that way. They proceeded past miniature electric Ferraris, inflatable rafts shaped like sea-serpents and a train set larger than their living room, complete with bridges and tunnels the little locomotive zipped through.

By the time they reached the second floor, he couldn't even respond to "Does Brian have any video games, Jeremy?"

"My son, the zombie," she muttered to herself and propelled him firmly toward the display. She figured her son's classmate must have the video unit already—was there a boy at St. Barnabas who didn't? So, a game cartridge should do—*Dinosaur World, Undersea Adventure*, or *Space Gladiators*?

Connie opted for the dinosaurs; if Brian already had that one, Mrs. Herman would just have to exchange it. Jeremy now had his nose glued to the display case and his breath was fogging the glass. She wedged a box under her purse arm and used the other one to guide her son into the line for the cashier.

"Well, hello there!" a familiar voice said behind them. Connie turned to face a large, plush panda bear. It was in the arms of Kenneth Considine. "This must be Jeremy," he added, looking down.

"Why, yes," she stammered, absolutely flabbergasted. It had never, ever occurred to her that they might meet by accident. And here, of all places! "Jeremy, say hello to Mr. Considine."

Amazingly, the boy snapped out of his deep trance. In fact, he was staring up at Ken with considerable interest—and critical intent. *Uh-oh,* his mother fretted, I should have guessed. *All the experts say it's only natural for a kid to resent a divorced parent's possible new partner. And Jeremy's smart enough to intuit how much I "like" this man. What do I do now?*

What she did was remain frozen until her son delivered a second surprise. After a lengthy scrutiny, he raised his right arm. "Hi, Ken. Whose bear is that?"

Ken disengaged an arm and shook Jeremy's extended hand.

"This is for my niece Belinda. She's just a little girl and she lives down South. What did *you* get?"

"Aw, we were only getting a birthday present. I'm going to a party."

Whoops! Constance hurriedly glanced at her watch. "Good grief—we've only got half an hour." Fishing in her purse for the credit card, she added to the cashier, "And this has to be gift-wrapped."

Ken peered at the box she held. "*Dinosaur Jungle*—that sounds real interesting."

"Uh-huh." Jeremy was acting as if *he* had selected the gift and his mother decided to let him get away with it. "Ricky Warren has that one and he likes it a lot. Are you going to take that bear down there yourself?"

"No, I have to send it. I can't go now—I'm very busy."

"You were in the treasure palace with Mom." He was chattering away as if they'd known each other for years. "You know that metal detector—the one Mom found the crown with?"

Ken grinned. "Yes, that was *your* detector. That was a terrific idea you had. All those jewels would still be hidden in the mansion if we hadn't had the machine."

Jeremy preened and kept on talking. "I got the idea from this TV show. . . ." His little voice filled the silence between the two adults as they made their way to the gift wrap counter. Ken was paying close attention to the narrative; Connie marveled that a man without children knew so well how to relate to one.

Now carrying colorful F.A.O. Schwarz shopping bags, the three of them made their way down the escalator and out to Fifth Avenue. The leaves of Central Park were just beginning their fall change, she noted, flashes of gold and scarlet tipping the greenery. Her mind was taking evasive action, trying to avoid the painful topic of how to say goodbye, when she felt a firm hand propelling her into a waiting taxi. Ken and her son, it seemed, had agreed to share a cab uptown. "Where does this Brian Herman live?" Ken was asking.

"Uh, Park and Sixty-Eighth."

"That'll be the first stop, driver." Ken climbed in beside her and Jeremy followed, still talking. The story of how Brian Herman came to have no front teeth—and the tremendous advantage this gave him when it came to spitting—got yet another airing.

"Your friend lives in a fancy house," Ken commented as the cab pulled up to an elaborate, canopied entrance.

In a flash, a waistcoated doorman wearing white gloves had the car door open. "Would this young gentleman be attending the party in the Herman residence?"

"Yes, he is," said Constance.

"Yes, I am," said Jeremy, climbing out.

"Ah, good. Ma'am, Mrs. Herman has asked me to inform the parents that she has engaged a car service to return the guests to their homes—it's so difficult to know exactly when the party will conclude, you see. Does the young man know his address?"

"Three-forty-three West End Avenue, Apartment 12-G," Jeremy contributed. "Phone, six-two-eight-three-two-one-one."

"Excellent." The doorman took the smaller shopping bag from the car and latched the door. "Do have a nice day." Connie and Ken looked at each other silently. He leaned forward toward the cab driver, "Madison and Seventy-Fifth."

She didn't dare believe it was happening, not until they had made it to his apartment door without seeing anyone they knew. The fact that his hands shook slightly, handling the keys, made it even more unreal.

Then—click!—they were inside. The foyer was small and shadowed. Even before the door had swung completely closed, she was in his arms and they were pressed together from head to toe. He was kissing her deeply, almost harshly, and the hardness of his muscled body pushed her back against the door. There was another, special hardness thrusting low on her stomach. She rocked her hips slightly from side to side to savor it, stimulate it even more.

"Ah, God, the way you do that," he whispered. "And the way I'm going to do this . . ." which was slip a hand up under her skirt and caress her delicately through the wisp of panty hose. Then his hand was tugging at the lace waistband.

He was panting. She could tell he was in urgent need of relief. Stepping out of his arms a bit, Connie slid the panty hose down. "Yes, now," she said and heard the sound of a zipper opening.

He moaned, and then his hands were under her skirt again, lifting her hips up, up and over his erection. She wrapped her legs around his waist and felt him slide home. He moved to pin her back against the door and pushed to penetrate even more deeply. A few thrusts and he exploded into orgasm, his whole body whip-lashing from the force. Connie held tight.

"Sorry about that." His breathing was slowing now and he kissed her forehead.

"Not to worry." She giggled. And meant it. Because if his sexual need was that great, if he climaxed that rapidly—well, a woman didn't have to be a great expert to guess that he hadn't been sleeping with anyone else.

"Your turn now," he murmured and walked her, still wrapped around him, into the bedroom. He laid her down on the bed—neatly made with a Navaho-style bedspread, she noted—and began to undress her properly, starting with scarf and jewelry. Connie lay back and enjoyed it as he smiled over her. "This is the first time I've taken a *skirt* off you." He tickled her tummy, pulling off the pink satin half-slip.

"Ooh-ooh, don't do that! I can't stand it!" She curled up in a ball, laughing. He tickled the back of her neck till she straightened out in reaction. In a flash, his head was at her breasts, his mouth nibbling and nipping in an excruciatingly stimulating way. When he had her moaning and writhing, his head went lower to complete the ecstasy.

Connie ran her fingers through Ken's hair as his tongue did unimaginable things to her... composure. Then she was at the top—the very peak of pleasure and falling....

"Asleep?" he was saying. "I make you fall asleep?"

Her eyes opened with a snap. "No! I . . . guess I sort of blacked out."

"Does this happen often?" He frowned.

"No. Never before. I think it's a tribute to your skill—I just couldn't take any more. I mean, that was the most . . ."

"Good." He smiled now and stretched out beside her, an arm under her head. "Let's just relax a bit."

"Whoa!" She reared up in alarm. "I don't know what time Jeremy will be getting home."

"Why don't you call the hosts . . ."

"The Hermans. Good idea." A rather harried woman's voice informed her over the din of twenty eight-year-olds that the party was still in the gift-opening phase, still had the meal and entertainment—a hired clown and magician—to go and would probably last another hour and a half.

"Good," said Ken. She could see that he was ready—completely ready—to make love again. Which they did.

18

THIS IS IT! Connie's brain announced noisily as she awoke. The Vernay sale begins at last! Not only would her long and arduous task be accomplished and her place at Villiers, Buck be confirmed, but she would be seeing her lover for the first time in three weeks, since the meeting in F.A.O. Schwarz. Though, she giggled, it was unlikely they'd be able to do what they'd done that day. As a courtesy to the museum that shared Augustine's bounty, Ian Buck had grudgingly agreed to invite several of its representatives to view the opening of this grand auction. Emilio Sant'Angelo would be coming with several curators and "that Considine fellow."

Naturally, none of them would be down on the selling floor with the ordinary bidders, collectors and dealers. For special guests there was a viewing room high overhead, lodged near the ceiling of the hall like a movie theater's projection booth. This plush little observation room was for the privileged few. Its walls were soft brocade, lit by crystal sconces. Its padded armchairs were in comfortable contrast to the rows of folding chairs below. A wide glass window afforded a fine view of the proceedings without intrusion.

Connie looked down at the auction room as people began to trickle in, edging their way gingerly through closely packed rows of seating. Requests for tickets to the Vernay sale far outnumbered the hall's usual capacity; Mr. Buck had ordered extra chairs jammed in every which way. No matter how rich or powerful the auction-goer, he or she would be squashed uncomfortably into place like the lowliest economy-class flier.

As they entered, the lucky ticket-holders signed in and got a bidding paddle—an object rather like the Ping-Pong instrument, except each paddle carried a big, black number painted on white. That number meant that no names had to be recorded during the sale; the bidder would just waggle the paddle in response to the auctioneer's call, signaling that he would meet the price.

But for those who *really* wanted to remain anonymous, there was a row of specially installed phones lining the hall's right-hand wall. These phones would be manned by delegates who would narrate the proceedings and transmit the wishes of shadowy participants. Constance knew all the reasons the wealthy would want to cloak themselves this way. One was security—why let an ambitious burglar know what could be gained by breaking into your home? Then there were ex-wives, and stockholders in your company, who would be enraged if they found out you had *that much* money to throw away on collecting. The same applied to royalty and elected officials who'd have to face furious tax-paying citizens. And for those with truly ill-gotten gains, there were always the looming twin specters of the Lawman and the Taxman.

Yet, Connie mused, these were the people who would go to any length, spend any sum, to get their hands on art treasures. And the joke was that the auction house almost always knew just who these "nameless" bidders were, despite all the attempts at secrecy. Villiers, Buck would hardly accept a bid for millions of dollars from a voice on the phone without knowing that the voice had the cash to back it up!

The sound of the door opening pulled her around, heart in throat. As a sentimental gesture only Kenneth Considine would understand, the red Chanel suit was her uniform of the day. She hoped he'd remember the outfit that began the Vernay adventure and now would end it.

An attendant held the door as the party filed in. Ian Buck had two special guests with him—a minor Saudi prince, who was connected to his bidding delegate down on the floor by walkie-talkie, and an actual cousin of the Queen. Did Her Majesty have eyes for the Petrov diadem? Connie wondered.

Then there was Emilio Sant'Angelo, suave in his Italian tailoring, kissing her hand. Behind him came a stunning redhead with a profile straight off an antique Roman coin. She was introduced as his wife—the third one, Connie knew—Adrianna. Then two studious-looking curators in tweeds, one male, one female, who were obviously dazzled by the excitement and glamour. And finally, towering over them, Kenneth Considine.

The physical impact of his presence was as powerful as the day she'd first seen him, at the reading of the will. It was a tremendous effort to keep a calm countenance and steady voice as they shook hands. "Hard to believe we ever finished the cataloguing, isn't it?" she asked for effect, hoping it sounded cool enough to fool the others, especially Ian Buck.

"Yes, indeed. And now the show begins." Only she could know that "show" was an epithet in his mouth. The sting of it snarled in her ears as they took their seats.

"Ahhh . . ." Ian Buck breathed. Cedric Grimsby, the chief auctioneer, was mounting the podium below. The hall was a sea of close-packed heads and shoulders. Beside the podium and stretching into the wings were cadres of aides who would bring forth and display each item as its turn came up on the block. Another group of assistants stood along the walls, ready to pick up any nod of the head or twitch of a numbered paddle that Grimsby might not detect.

"Ladies and gentlemen, welcome." Cedric Grimsby was, naturally, British and his accent was even more baroque than his employer's. He made a graceful little speech about what a historic day this was. At least, that was what it sounded like to Connie, who could only understand about one word in three.

But there was no misunderstanding Cedric when he barked out names and numbers. "Our first offering of the day, Lot Number One, is this magnificent Caravaggio." He waved a hand at a richly colored canvas depicting a young courtier with a lute. "Do I have twenty million dollars?"

The crowd gasped at the bravado of it—to start the day with such a dazzling piece and such a high figure! There was a beat of silence, of inactivity. Then the first paddle peeked above the heads around it. "Do I have twenty million, two?" Grimsby said in a flash, meaning two hundred thousand dollars more.

The Sale of the Century was off and running. Constance looked around the observation room, where all eyes but hers were glued to the glass and the spectacle below. Ian Buck was breathing fast and looked like a man in the throes of sexual ecstasy. Beyond him, Ken lounged casually, his expression slightly bored and definitely disgusted.

Buck had been right—the Vernay scandal, the story of infidelity, embezzlement and murder—had *made* the auction. Those lucky enough to get tickets flaunted them and some losers—whom Ian Buck suspected just wanted to come for the show, not to buy—actually left town rather than have their disgrace known. Now the waves of bidding swept higher and higher, breaking all previous records and even the auction house's most optimistic estimates.

A silver-gilt and crystal epergne which once graced Madame du Barry's table—seven hundred and eighty thousand dollars! An ink study-sketch for Andrea del Sarto's *Holy Family*,—two million, fifteen thousand!

A minor Goya portrait of a Spanish noble he obviously didn't like—more than twenty million! It was like a feeding frenzy, with the taste of acquisition and the fever of big numbers goading the pack. The atmosphere in the hall was giddy and unreal.

As the morning swept on, Ian Buck made a crucial decision. "No break for lunch," he decreed. Connie knew why. If the bidding was halted, the hall emptied and everyone went out to eat, this fever might dissipate. Smarter to keep the crowd dynamics throbbing as they were. "Call those caterers, what's-their-name..."

"Elysian Meals," she supplied.

"Yes, yes," he said gesturing airily to a secretary who'd been summoned to the observation room by buzzer. "Tell them we need box lunches, their best, for—" he gave a shrewd glance at the hall below, "—oh, seven hundred. By one o'clock, Laurel." He turned back to the window without registering the expression on Laurel's face, which was one of horror. Connie gave her a sympathetic wink and smile. Because Sasha, the temperamental owner of Elysian Meals, would undoubtedly take out his wrath about this last-minute order on the hapless secretary. Seven hundred meals in less than two hours! Laurel slunk out of the box, pad and pencil in hand.

The high-energy spectacle of bidding and buying was so compelling that Constance was jolted by the sound of tea carts wheeling a meal into the privileged little room. This was no cold boxed lunch, but rather a refined menu prepared in Villiers, Buck's own kitchen by Ian Buck's personal chef. Down below, it was obvious that Sasha and his Elysian Meals had come through. The company's distinctive pink-and-mauve boxes were being passed around and seized eagerly by the crowd. Beverage carts stocked with everything from sparkling water to sparkling champagne squeezed their way along narrow, clogged aisles. Cedric Grimsby had taken a break and was replaced by his second-in-command. But the bidding and buying went on without a pause.

Up above, it was almost funny to see how eagerly the visitors from the New York tucked into the salmon mousse, buttery-tender filet mignon and radicchio salad. The Museum's cafeteria was famous—or rather, infamous—in art circles. It was common wisdom that the most edible items dispensed over its stainless steel counters were ham sandwiches and containers of yogurt. So it was understandable that the two curators quietly went back to the carts for seconds of the filet. Connie caught Ken's eye as he headed for a *third* piece of beef. Despite herself, she grinned.

Lord, what if Mr. Buck saw that? No problem, he was bending over the food himself. In an uncharacteristic gesture, he was filling a plate for the Saudi prince and serving it personally. *No, wait,* there was a motive. The Prince was whispering softly, liquidly into his walkie-talkie. Nothing should slow the torrents of money flowing through the auction hall, not even for a moment!

Rising to serve herself, Connie observed that Emilio Sant'Angelo and Wife Number Three were engaged in a heated, if muffled, argument. Adrianna was pointing at an item in the sale catalogue and whispering vociferously. Even in a foreign tongue, her desire to bid—to acquire—was crystal clear. Just as clear was that Emilio didn't want her to. *Hmm,* the thought came unbidden, *I wonder what Number Four will be like?* With difficulty, she turned to look through the window again, forcing her eyes away from the magnetic sight of her lover.

By four o'clock, it had become more than she could stand. The repeated rushes of adrenaline had worn off as treasures were brought to the podium, displayed and then whisked away again to the march of very large numbers. The popping up and down of bidding paddles was giving her a headache. The steady drain of tension probably contributed to the pounding in her skull, the fear that she would let it show—the love and lust she felt for the man sitting at the other end of the box.

"Mr. Buck," Connie whispered. Her boss nodded without turning his gaze from the mesmerizing scene of money being made. "If you'll excuse me for a bit . . ."

"Certainly, certainly." He leaned over to the Queen's cousin as if dismissing Connie's presence. "Rather a nice little pair of marquetry tables by Boulle coming next," he murmured invitingly.

On the way to the elevator, fatigue swept her entire body like a giant wave. Refuge was the goal—some peace and quiet in that handsome corner office. *Just close the door behind you and try to wipe your mind clear. Relax and unwind, maybe catch a few winks. Make a mental escape curled up comfortably in the armchair.*

It seemed like only seconds later that someone was knocking. Couldn't they leave her alone for a while, just a little while? She had to force the words out. "Come in."

The door swung open to reveal... Kenneth Considine.

Without knowing or thinking, Connie sprang out of the chair and into his arms. Surrounded by the sweet familiarity of his embrace, she lost track of time. So she had no idea how much later it was that the door opened again, this time without warning. Silhouetted in the frame was the narrow form of Ian Buck.

19

THE OFFICE WASN'T officially open yet, but her phone was beeping insistently. She cleared her throat and picked up the receiver with a trembling hand. "Constance Nathan here."

"Gooooood morning, Mrs. Nathan," purred Neville Edmiston. "Mr. Buck wants you here in his office." That was to let her know that *he* Neville, was being confided in by Ian Buck. "Directly. You're to bring the Guinzberg file with you." Copycatting his boss, Neville hung up abruptly.

This is it, my girl, she told herself. As the most senior vice president of the company, Neville had no doubt expected to manage the prized Vernay sale himself—only to have it snatched out of his grasp by the most junior, and only female, vice president. Now he would have his revenge and get to run the rest of the auction, with all the hard work and preparation handed to him on a platter! Plus, it seemed, he was going to inherit Mr. Guinzberg as a personal client. How nasty old Neville was going to love it all!

So stiffen your spine, Constance, and comport yourself with as much dignity as possible. Do your best to save poor Dennis's job; right now he must be shaking from the message you left on his answering ma-

chine. "I'm in real serious trouble, Dennis. I mean, deep water. I suggest you stay away from me and my office today. And stay away from Mr. Buck!" If Dennis hid out for a while, maybe Mr. Buck would forget whose assistant he'd been and spare *his* head.

Above all, she further admonished herself, don't let them see how much this is going to hurt—emotionally as well as financially. "I've put so much hard work into this job!" one side of her mind wailed, "it's not fair." The other side said firmly, "As John F. Kennedy observed, *life* is unfair. Let's get this over with."

Walking the corridors of Villiers, Buck for what she knew was the last time, it was obvious that the tom-toms of corporate rumor had been beating hard and fast. Ian Buck never hesitated to let everyone—everyone still in his good graces, that is—know when someone was about to get the sack, and why. Men and women who yesterday had greeted Constance Nathan with warmth seemed to pull away from her physically today. I might as well be wearing one of those leper's bells from the Middle Ages, she thought grimly, and be crying "Unclean! Unclean" as I go.

Neville Edmiston was holding the door to Buck's office open with obvious, supercilious relish. "I'll take that," he said, pointing to the accordion file labeled "Guinzberg," which was tucked under her arm. She handed it over meekly.

Ian Buck was sitting in the buff-leather chair behind his desk, but it was turned away, toward the full-length oil portrait of his father that dominated the room. All

Connie could see was the back of his head with its slicked-back hair. In the silence, Connie wondered if the story was true—had Humphrey Buck really driven his partner Ewan Villiers to suicide?

The chair spun around and she faced the icy visage of Buck, Junior. *Say nothing!* she ordered herself. She didn't.

After a pause—was he waiting for her to blubber, to confess?—the Briton broke the silence. "You have disappointed me, Constance."

"How, sir?"

"How?" His voice cracked. He was almost screeching, and rose up out of his chair, face reddened. "How? By rutting around with that Considine fellow when you were supposed to be taking care of *our* business!"

How dare he use such a word as 'rutting?' It was getting harder to keep her dignity. "If you look at the record, Mr. Buck, you will see I did take care of our business. I secured the major portion of the Vernay estate for sale and arranged the largest auction this house has ever conducted. May I go now?"

"Go?" It was almost a snort. "You're not going anywhere."

Constance blinked. "You mean I'm not fired?"

Ian Buck calmed down visibly. He smiled, enjoying her astonishment. "No, you are still employed by Villiers, Buck. You have too many contacts and too much expertise for us to dispense with your services. Mr. Guinzberg, for instance, refuses to deal with anyone else."

Holy cow! Was she going to get out of this with a whole coat?

The next words dashed her hope. "But of course we can no longer trust you to operate by yourself. You will be reporting to Neville," he continued smoothly, "and your salary will be reduced accordingly."

"Mr. Buck, if you agree that I did a good job . . ."

He cut her off with an abrupt gesture. "That's as may be. You have lost my confidence."

Unprepared for this scenario, this surprising turn of events, she stood rooted to the spot. Until Neville stuck the opened Guinzberg file under her nose; he was almost leering. "And the first thing you'll do for me, today, is reorganize this entire catalogue to fit *my* format."

LOOKING BACK it was as if somebody else had stepped in and done it. Certainly the career-wise Constance Fischer Nathan, who had made so many sacrifices for her position, would never have pulled such a stunt. But this other woman didn't care. She was mad as hell and wasn't going to take it anymore. "Mad as hell," she repeated aloud on Park Avenue. A few pedestrians looked at her as if she were crazy and walked on.

Now what do you do, Constance? How do you tell Jeremy we can't afford St. Barnabas's tuition any more, so, starting next semester, it's off to public school? How do you ask Bob Nathan for money to live on, at least till you get another job? And who in the art community will hire you, after this? Why did you do it?

What she had done was calmly accept the Guinzberg file from Neville Edmiston, who was shorter than she was, tear it in two, right through the sturdy canvas and cardboard, smack Neville in the face with one half and hurl the remainder at the head of Ian Buck, who sat there with pieces of paper sticking to his shoulders while she spoke—yelled, actually, loud enough for everybody on the floor to hear.

"Lost your *confidence*, have I, Ian?" she yelled. It was the first and only time she'd addressed him by his baptismal name. It felt good. "Ian *baby*? After I spend months in that pigsty of a mansion and run the biggest and best sale this joint has ever had? Well, that's a laugh! Confidence from slime like you is something I can do without. And you can take this job and shove it."

Then she'd stormed down the hall, past the astonished faces of staffers peering from each office. Next stop was her former quarters, to quickly make a muddle of the files. Let Neville spend a few months straightening them out! she thought fiercely, stalking out onto the street, where she threw her Villiers, Buck ID card down a storm sewer.

She was raising her hand to hail a cab when it hit—taxis were a luxury the unemployed could not afford. The thing to do was go to the corner and take a bus home. If only she could stop shaking all over, as if absorbing blows.

Steady, steady. Let's just walk a bit. There, that's better—only wait a minute. This direction you're walking, Constance, isn't toward the crosstown bus. You're headed uptown. Walking rather fast, actually, up Fifth Avenue. Straight for the New York Museum of Art. And Kenneth Considine, who will no doubt remind you how he said all along that you were working in a dirty business, and employed by a creep.

The white marble bulk of the museum still feels familiar from visits with family and friends. And remember the outings led by the art instructor at Miss Whitney's? Now, as an adult, you can only feel profound pity for poor Miss Quinley, trying to impart culture to a pack of giggling teenagers. Too bad you haven't had time for a visit to the New York since you got married. First there was that awful investment-banking job and then there was Jeremy. Spare time was always tighly scheduled. And you knew that, one of these days, the teachers at St. Barnabas would bring your son and his classmates here.

Well, you've got plenty of spare time now, Constance. It was a grim thought as she climbed the imperious rank of marble steps, lined as usual with rows of sitting tourists.

Inside, the ceilings were sky-high. They swallowed up the noise so that the atmosphere was slightly hushed, almost religious. People from all over and all walks of life milled around the central hall and eddied out into the maze of corridors extending in every direction. A large pack of Japanese tourists, cameras lashed around their necks, trotted obediently behind a tour guide.

At the information desk sat several women of prosperous mien and a certain age. Volunteers, Connie registered. She joined the line of questioners and heard these ladies respond to "Where do I find the Egyptian stuff?"... "How do I get tickets to the Versailles exhibit?" and, inevitably, "Where are the restrooms?"

Now she was at the head of the line. If she said she was looking for Kenneth Considine they'd probably ask if she had an appointment. Better, "Could you tell me where the administrative offices are?"

The volunteer eyed her in a maternal manner. "My, we're all dressed up for the job interview." She smiled. Connie flushed. "Here, I'll show you." The woman tore a map of the building from a huge pad of them and traced a path in red ink. "Good luck!"

"Thanks, I can use it." Peering at the map, she went through the Hall of Armor, turned left at Persian Statuary, and took the staircase in the middle of Burmese temple sculptures. As she got nearer her goal, her knees started acting up again. So much so that by the time Constance reached Museum Offices—Please Check In she had to hold on to the reception desk.

"May I help you?"

"Is Mr. Considine in?"

"Who shall I say is visiting?"

"Constance Nathan."

The receptionist blinked. She knew the name; of course, people here would have been just as fascinated with the Vernay Collection as the auctioneers. "Mrs. Nathan is here to see you?" she asked the intercom.

The machine squawked and crackled back—hopelessly antiquated, Connie thought—you couldn't even tell if it was a male or female voice. But the message was what she wanted to hear. "That way, please, Mrs. Nathan. At the end of the hall. Mr. Considine is on the phone."

It was a supreme effort to walk calmly and not run all the way down the corridor lined with old-fashioned office doors. A single one was placed squarely in the end wall and its rippled-glass pane was lettered in gold, Mr. Considine. It was ajar. She gave it a push.

He was in shirtsleeves, feet upon the desk and phone clenched to an ear. The other hand waved her in and toward the couch. But his attention was elsewhere. "No, no! Mrs. Ryder, I'm certainly not suggesting that we cancel the exhibit—just postpone it until the budget can be accommodated from operating revenues."

Well, no wonder he wasn't paying attention to Constance Nathan. He was talking to Wilhelmina Ryder, née Profitt. As in Profitt Oil Company of Tulsa. Mrs. Ryder was one of the museum's most generous benefactors and had recently joined the board of the New York. Ken was clearly trying to charm some cash out of her, right now.

After that, Connie's mind went blank for the rest of the conversation. Next thing she knew, Ken was addressing her. "Did he fire you?"

"No."

Oddly enough, the answer seemed to displease him. "Then why are you here instead of at the sale?"

Her mouth was dry and it took a while to frame the words. "Because I quit."

"You *what*?" He shot upright in the chair.

"I quit. Ian Buck chewed me out, which I expected. He said he no longer had confidence in me, which I expected. Then he busted me down to assistant again, cut my pay *and* told me I had to work for Neville Edmiston, who's the nastiest guy in the whole organization. So I blew my cork and told him to take the job and shove it." She hung her head abashedly. "And I threw things and destroyed my files."

"You threw things?" Ken tossed his head and laughed heartily. "That's terrific!"

"What's so terrific about my being out of a job?"

"Now we can get married."

This time it really happened; her knees gave way and she landed on the floor in a heap.

20

"THREE P.M., doors open to Senior Benefactors and their guests only. Seating in the Vernay Wing. 4:00 p.m., the ceremony. Four-thirty, reception and cocktails. 6:00 p.m., doors open to Individual and Corporate Patrons for viewing and the buffet dinner is served. Nine o'clock, general admission to Museum members with tickets and media." Emilio Sant'Angelo's assistant was reading the schedule aloud as he followed him down the corridor at full gallop.

They screeched to a halt under an archway swathed in colorful bunting. Three workmen were struggling to mount a large plaque above it; the wood was painted to look like marble and The Vernay Collection was lettered in gold. Below that, only slightly smaller, Presentation Courtesy of a Gift from Mrs. Dennison Ryder.

"What? Why is the sign not up already?" Sant'Angelo was working himself into a fine tantrum. "Did I not tell you yesterday the sign *must* be in place for the photographers?"

The workmen remained calm. The senior among them, pulling on a guywire, said "Yes, Mr. Sant'Angelo. But you also had us change the lettering from 'Wilhelmina' to 'Mrs. Dennison.' The gold paint didn't dry till just now."

"Ridiculous!" the director sputtered. "Nothing goes right! Make sure there is a spotlight on that sign. Make that two spotlights—one from above, one from below." He was off and running again, pursued by the faithful assistant. Behind them, the three men rolled their eyes and grinned.

Beyond the arch was a world of splendor and enchantment. Financed by Wilhelmina Ryder, an entire wing of the New York's original, main building had been gutted and redesigned for the exhibition. Under its arched glass roof, velvet-covered partitions broke the vast space into viewing areas. On one side was the recreation of a salon in Venice, when that city ruled the oceans, its sea-green walls gently complementing the glow of gilded furniture and sparkling mirrors. Beyond it was a corner devoted to Russian furniture and bibelots, set off by a vibrant red wall-covering. And along one entire long wall, Augustine de Vernay's porcelains were represented, hanging in artful arrangements on vanilla-colored watered silk.

But Emilio Sant'Angelo passed most of this quickly, with only a few imprecations and supplications flung at the staff—who were busy with last-minute adjustments and burnishing. He and his assistant zipped down to the far end of the wing, where rows of folding chairs faced a podium draped in yellow brocade.

The director stopped and pressed his hands together, eyeing the scene intently. "Candelabra," he said after a bit. "We need candles here, definitely—for the soft glow, do you see? The Rensselaer set from my office will do quite nicely, no?" He cocked his head, visualizing. "Yes, the Rensselaers." Someone went off to fetch them.

Now a parade of young men and women were entering, bearing pots and vases and armfuls of flowers. "Aha, so here we have the Floral Splendor," Emilio observed. Ordinarily, the Museum could not afford Manhattan's priciest florist, but Wilhelmina Ryder and her checkbook made all things possible. "You had better not have put any Baby's Breath in there," Sant'-Angelo added sternly. "Filthy stuff!" He clucked over the bouquets for a few moments and then went back to brooding over the podium, adjusting the now present Rensselaer candelabra.

He stepped back for a longer view. "The lady *is* wearing mandarin yellow, is she not?"

"Yes, she is," a voice answered from overhead.

The Director's head snapped back in the direction of the voice. A look of pure horror crossed his face. "Kenneth! What in the hell are you doing up there?"

"Just tinkering with the lighting." Considine's head appeared over the top of the partition. "The Van Eyck still isn't right."

"Get down from there this very instant!" It was a full-throated scream. "What are you, a crazy man? You are getting married today. For lighting we have electricians, technical people . . ."

"Calm yourself, Emilio." The head vanished from sight. "There's still plenty of time."

"These two are insane!" Sant'Angelo addressed the world at large, waving his arms. "The groom is playing with . . . lamps and already I find *her* in the office fooling around with a computer—the bride!"

A laugh floated over the partition.

"Out! Out of here. Go home. Get dressed. Out!"

"Okay, okay. The lighting's pretty good now, anyway." The sound of Kenneth Considine's footsteps receded into the distance.

WHAT THE BRIDE herself was doing at that moment would no doubt have scandalized the romantic Emilio Sant'Angelo even more. First he had shooed her out of her office at the museum. Then her best friend and her babysitter had shooed her out of her own apartment. Bird Salter and Amelia Wickes were setting everything up at home for a casual wedding reception that would be held after the formal one at the New York. They made it clear that she, Constance, was just in the way. Then Bob Salter had taken Jeremy and his own kids to the World Trade Center for some sky-high sightseeing and a fun lunch.

The yellow silk suit was pressed. The bouquet was in the refrigerator. Her nails and hair were done.

So the bride-to-be was sitting on a bench in Central Park, watching the colorful carousel and listening to its authentic steam calliope cheerfully pump out tunes. She lunched elegantly on a hot dog and soda from the nearest pushcart, and did plenty of thinking about what had occurred since the day she'd collapsed on the floor of Ken's office.

He had picked her up, laughing, and set her solicitously on the cracked old leather couch. "Why are you so surprised, Connie? And by the way, do you accept my proposal?"

"You never said a word!" she cried accusingly. "About marriage or the future or anything. I figured you were just having a fling."

"You should know me better than that." He sat on the arm of the couch and held her hand. "I'm a serious kind of guy."

"But you never said *anything*," she repeated stubbornly.

"Constance, Constance. There is no way I could be married to somebody who's on the other side of the fence, professionally speaking. That whole scene really sickens me."

Aha! So that was the *gray spot* you were looking for! a voice spoke inside her head. The Man of Principle saw you as some kind of Marked Woman Who Sells Art to the Rich. "Well, no problem now, huh? Since I no longer have a profession?"

"I'm sure we can work something out here. But I'm getting kind of tired of asking—will you marry me?"

"Give me a break!" Connie replied with her usual subtlety. "Of course I will!"

Since then it had been remarkably smooth sailing. Ken had marched her directly into Emilio Sant'Angelo's office and informed the thrilled Director that a) she was no longer with Villiers, Buck and b) they were getting married. Emilio informed them with many flights of verbal fancy that he was taking over the nuptials. This was both for sentimental reasons—"Ah! The romance! I sensed it, my dears, I could just *feel* the bond between you!" he'd claimed—and professional ones. "Think, just think of it. What a spectacle! A marriage to open the Vernay Exhibition, right in the gallery. The late Marquise's ghost causes a great love to be consummated over the ashes of her own love. No one will ever have a pageant such as this. The press will go simply wild!"

That last sentence had made Constance nervous; she knew what it was like to have the press interested in you. But she could hardly turn the director down, because he also solved the unemployment problem—after clapping his hands with glee at hearing just how Constance Nathan had tendered her resignation to Ian Buck. Sant'Angelo pointed out that the chief financial officer of the New York was planning to retire; it was high time to bring in a successor. "Who better?" he asked, waving at Constance. "Of course, we do not have the, um, salary resources of an auction house . . ." he added tentatively.

"I accept anyway," she replied loudly. "Mr. Sant'Angelo, you're so very kind . . ."

Her new boss cut her off. "Nonsense, nonsense, dear lady. And to you I will always be, please, Emilio."

The emotional roller-coaster of the day took its toll as she and Ken walked, hand in hand, back to his office. "Wow! I'm really beat."

Her brand-new fiancé put a supportive arm around her shoulder. "Let me take you home." A certain glint in his eye indicated that he had more than transportation in mind. What a delicious idea! But...

"Uh, listen. I'd love to. Only Mrs. Wickes—that's Jeremy's sitter—isn't feeling well. I promised I'd pick him up early. And I think I'd better break the news to him, uh, alone, if you don't mind?"

Ken hugged her shoulder. "Right, of course." They contented themselves with a long kiss on the steps of the museum, as he put her into a cab. She rehearsed the speech to her son on the way across the park. Sure, Jeremy seemed to like Ken when they met, but how would he like him as a stepfather? She'd heard some horror stories from friends who had remarried—children who refused to obey the new "parent," who acted out their negative feelings, even did their best to sabotage the marriage.

What would she, Constance, do if the two males in her life didn't get along? "Kill myself," was the only answer she could come up with. She ran the speech through in her mind while preparing dinner—that old favorite, lasagna, just to be on the safe side.

"Jeremy, I have some news."

"Uh-huh."

"I changed jobs today. I'm going to be working at a museum—you know what a museum is. I think I won't have to work such long hours any more. And—" deep breath "—I'm getting married."

Her son chewed lasagna in silence for a few suspense-filled moments. A little bit of tomato sauce was on his cheek, but she decided not to mention it. "To Ken?" he asked, finally.

"Yes, to Ken."

"Oh." Another bite and chewing. "When?"

"Pretty soon. There's going to be a big party."

"Oh." And that was all her son said on the subject until that Saturday, when Ken was coming by for a formal get-acquainted visit. Was his silence a good sign or bad? Should she press him for a response? Better not. Give him time to get used to the idea.

But Saturday she was pretty shaky. Bless him, the stepfather-to-be seemed quite at ease. In his casual uniform of Levis and cowboy boots, he kissed her at the door and said, "Where's Jeremy?"

At the sound, a little head peeked out the bedroom doorway. Man and boy stared at each other down the hall for what seemed, to Connie anyway, like an eternity. Then her son marched down the hall, stuck out his hand and said, "Hi again, Ken." In five minutes, they were discussing baseball and by midafternoon Jeremy had revealed his thoroughly revolting secret recipe, involving marshmallows, American cheese and a microwave oven.

During the weeks when Ken and Emilio Sant'Angelo and almost everybody else at the New York were toiling away to get the Vernay Exhibition ready, Connie was finding out that the museum's financial department was even more out-of-date than the one at Villiers, Buck had been. Only this morning she'd been introducing her staff to "This new thing, a computer," when the director rousted her from the office with exclamations of horror about the violation of wedding etiquette.

Working for Emilio was definitely an improvement over working for Ian Buck, she mused, even if the pay wasn't as good. Emilio got a second chance to prove his kindness shortly after hiring her. It took her former employer several days to remember that Constance Nathan had had an assistant, and to find him. Dennis had taken her advice and laid low. But find him, and fire him, Buck did. She was somehow embarrassed to ask, but Ken assured her Sant'Angelo "would love to get Ian Buck's goat." Dennis Morton was duly put on the Museum payroll and assigned to the Special Events department. Funnily enough, that was the section that was managing the wedding!

She was jolted out of her reverie by a squirrel. This time of year most of them were in a nut-burying frenzy. One fat and sassy fellow, though, had noticed the new food source sitting on the bench. Obligingly, she broke off a piece of hot-dog bun and tossed it to him. The little animal sat back on his tail and held the bread between both paws, nibbling away busily.

Wasn't it ironic? she thought, sinking back into reverie. All those months in the mansion, when they were supposed to be antagonists, they had plenty of time alone to themselves. And now that they were supposed to be lovers, there was hardly a second of solitude! So much was going on that their contact had been limited to a few words of tenderness, a quick kiss behind an office door, a whispered good-night over the phone.

Except, of course, Constance giggled at the thought, for the "packing" they'd done last Sunday. It was triggered by an unexpected invitation for Jeremy to go to the circus with Brian Herman. The boys were getting to be good friends and Connie noted with relief that two little white stubs were finally emerging in the front of Brian's mouth. She was also flattered when Mrs. Herman confided she was "happy to see Brian playing with Jeremy, who has such nice manners."

Brian's apartment was near St. Barnabas and a couple of afternoons a week Jeremy would stop off there rather than with Mrs. Wickes. It was always convenient, because the Hermans had a formal staff of servants; Jeremy was picking up words like "butler."

Anyway, last Sunday the impromptu circus invitation for Jeremy had come. His mother had been working on her new computer, tracking the New York's cash flow and itemizing a list of wedding gifts with the names and addresses of donors. As she knew from her first marriage, woe betide the bride who thanks Aunt Matilda for the embroidered placemats when they actually came from Cousin Edna!

Ken was finally starting to pack in his apartment. They had agreed, almost without discussion, that he would simply move in with her and Jeremy. There was plenty of space—or at least, plenty of space by Manhattan standards—and Ken said he felt more comfortable on the casual West Side. But it was just a week till the wedding, and he had packed nothing at all. Right after they got back from the honeymoon on St. Maarten, he was supposed to vacate. Connie didn't want to nag, but . . . "Okay, okay," Ken said. "I'll pack Sunday."

"Brian's going to the circus and he wants to know can I come too?" Jeremy clearly was hoping for an affirmative answer.

Hmm. This was too good a chance to pass up. "We're on our way," his mother replied, grabbing her purse and a jacket. She dropped Jeremy off on Park Avenue and directed the cabbie to Madison.

The doorman recognized her. "Oh, yes, I'll buzz Mr. Considine."

"Please don't. I'd like to surprise him." The doorman looked dubious, but eventually agreed that no, Constance did not look like a burglar or mugger and yes, she could go upstairs unannounced.

She rang the doorbell and heard a very grumpy voice yell, "Coming!" Then there was a crash. "Damn!" said the same voice. Footsteps, and the door was yanked open.

"Hi!" she said brightly. "I came to help you pack."

"Pack?"

"Uh-huh."

Before she knew it, he'd grabbed one wrist and her waist and slung her over his shoulder. "I've got a much better idea." He headed for the bedroom, weaving his way through a cluster of half-filled cartons. They landed together on the bed, bouncing and laughing. The first kiss was soft and warm as they lay facing each other. "How long can you stay?"

"Till five. Jeremy's gone to the circus with a friend."

"Good." Another kiss, a little harder, this time with his hand behind her head, twining in her hair. "Then we don't have to hurry."

"Nope." She leaned on one elbow and kissed the side of his neck, right where the pulse was. The way she knew he liked it, with little nips of the teeth. The pulse beat harder and faster. She pulled the neck of his sweatshirt down a bit and nibbled on the shoulder, breathing in the scent of a man becoming aroused. "Mmm, you taste good."

"Let's see how tasty *you* are today." Now he had her rolled over on her back and she could feel the sweet weight of his body, pressing from the waist down. She spread her legs and he slid in between them. Through the fabric there was that virile, thrilling thrust; she moved her hips to enjoy it. "Ahh," was all he said, but he moved the same way. And they were breathing the same way, too, slow and deep. No, he was not in a hurry today.

They stayed at this delicious plateau for some time. It got her so hot and bothered that she felt slightly damp all over. Slightly moist, especially there, where he was pushing against her with a steady, riding rhythm. She raised her knees a bit to make the feeling even better, even closer to the edge.

Whew! That was almost too good; she'd nearly gone on ahead of him, so to speak. Time for a little retaliatory action . . . unbutton the blouse, let him get a peek inside it. Make sure he sees how hard he's made her nipples, obvious through the mauve lace of the bra. Then, with a stripperlike flourish, unhook the bra . . .

Oh, yes, he was looking all right. As the cups released her breasts, the smooth action of his hips suddenly bucked. And stopped. "Something wrong?"

He was breathing through gritted teeth. "I almost . . ." he grinned.

"Me too, back there a bit."

He was backing off her, standing up. The way his phallus was pressing against the fly of his pants, vividly revealing its contours and size, she could guess he must be in pain. "Why don't you . . . open up?" She smiled lasciviously.

"Do it for me. I'll enjoy that more."

His costume for packing was a University of Louisville sweatshirt and cutoff jeans. The zipper was old and it was under a lot of pressure from what was behind it. Gently, she tugged, fearful of causing him more pain. And tugged again. And there was no layer of underwear in the way, either. "Did you know I was coming?" Giggle.

"Nope—just lucky."

She slid the cutoffs down over his hips as he pulled off the sweatshirt. She admired. She knew that some women didn't like to look at naked men, particularly naked men in the engorged, fully aroused, pulsing state Ken was in. But she, Constance, liked it. Especially when she knew what the man was going to do to her. She touched herself in anticipation.

"Mmm." Ken advanced, his hands now busy. Soon, she was as clothesless as he, and he was laying her down on the bed. *Soooo* nicely. It was like floating on a warm sea, to open your eyes and look up into the face of your beloved—that gorgeous face. He enters and all is perfect. Perfect...

"Well, it's your fault," Ken said sometime later.

"*What*'s my fault?"

"You interrupted my packing—just as I was really getting into it, too."

Connie sat up and looked around. The bedroom—the entire apartment—was liberally strewn with cardboard cartons and various types of luggage. But the contents of the apartment had hardly been touched at all. "Hmph," she said. "A fine packer you are."

"Actually, I thought I was rather good." He was looking quite smug and was obviously referring to something else.

She laughed and smacked him lightly on the bottom. "Bad boy! What time is it?"

"4:10."

"Well, let's get some clothes on, right away, and see how much we can polish off before five."

He groaned. "Do we have to?"

"Kenneth Considine, let me refresh your memory! We are getting married in one week. Do you want to come back from the honeymoon and find your possessions out in the street?"

Really, men could be so unsensible. "Which cartons are for books?"

"Uh—I hadn't really gotten that far."

Growling slightly under her breath, Connie seized a pen and wrote on the side of one carton Books—1. Under her firm direction Ken emptied the bedroom bookshelves into it. In an hour, they accomplished more than he had all day. But it was the hour *before* the packing that she would remember. . .

THE SQUIRREL was still sitting on its haunches, hoping for more largess. "Whoa!" It started and ran away at the sound of a bride discovering it was much later than she'd realized. She took off across the park, running in a most unbridelike manner.

From then on, the time passed as if in a dream. Next thing she knew, a string quartet was playing and a hall full of very chic people was turning to look at her. All around there were familiar objects in an unfamiliar setting. That Venetian mirror, for instance. She remembered it hanging, covered with grime, in a bedroom; now it sparkled in a salon suite. And those gorgeous malachite end tables—they looked much larger than they had when piled up in a haystack of furniture!

That flash of light was a reflection off a TV camera lens. Reporters were scribbling in notebooks, too; Emilio had really pulled out all the stops. Every time another item appeared about the Nathan/Considine nuptials, he cackled with glee, imagining how furious Ian Buck must be.

There was Emilio, in the front row by the yellow-draped podium. And that yellow matched her suit perfectly. One of his touches, no doubt. Yes, he was beaming with paternal pride. And beside him the flame-haired Adrianna. Nice to know their marriage had survived the Vernay Auction Crisis.

Then came Dennis Morton, looking officious as the head usher, seating the guests according to a plan he consulted with great seriousness. As usual, he was a fashion plate in striped morning trousers and cutaway coat. Connie winked at him as he passed.

Aha—the music was picking up tempo and volume. The groom's party was entering. Leading the way was Jeremy; he'd been so thrilled when she asked him if he'd like to be ring-bearer! He was wearing his new navy-blue suit and a huge, proud smile. *Let's hope he remembered the ring.* Somebody had combed his hair to a state of neatness that was truly astounding.

The best man was a fraternity brother of Ken's named Ron Brownridge. Ron had been very quiet when they met and was obviously studying Constance intently. She apparently passed whatever test Ron had been giving her; after about six giant-size beers he confided, "Lacey McCally is the biggest bitch I ever met—'scuse my language—and I was afraid Ken was makin' another mistake." Connie struggled to smother the laugh.

Enter the groom himself. Her heart melted yet again to see him, the man she wanted more than anything in life. *Wow.* She'd never seen him in a dinner jacket before, and probably never would again. Emilio Sant'Angelo practically had to beg him to wear anything more dressy than a suit for the occasion. How had she caught such a prize? "Thank you, Augustine de Vernay!" she whispered to herself.

"This is it!" Barbara Salter muttered, giving her a nudge. The music was shifting into a processional. Bird had elected to wear what she called "matron-of-honor beige." Actually, it was a lovely lace sheath that set off her hair and tan nicely as she moved down the aisle.

Whoops! Now everybody had turned to look at her and the string quartet was sawing away at top volume. The dreamlike feeling was stronger than ever.

Constance floated through the sea of people in a daze until she reached the podium. A judge stood behind it—a very important judge, she'd been told. Here was her beloved joining her.

The details of the ceremony didn't really penetrate but she guessed she was saying the right words at the right time because things seemed to be progressing smoothly. It was only when Ken reached to Jeremy for the ring that she looked down and snapped out of it.

Down there on the floor, where they were standing, those colors and patterns rang a bell. Was it . . . could it be?

The judge had gotten to the part that goes "By the authority vested in me . . ." and she looked up into her about-to-be-husband's eyes questioningly. Then, trying not to show any expression, she rolled her eyes toward their feet.

Leaning down, he whispered, "Yup, it *is* our Qum. I'm a sentimental guy," and kissed her. The applause of the guests rang sweetly in Constance's ears. . . .

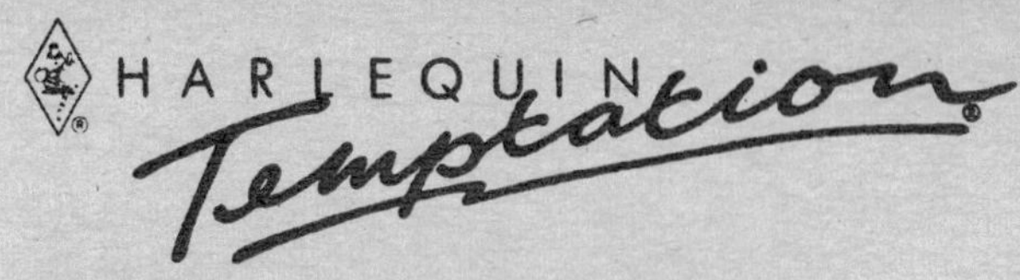

COMING NEXT MONTH

#301 SATISFACTION GUARANTEED Judith McWilliams

Kiley Sheridan, a teacher of the learning disabled, wanted her graduating students to find jobs. Max Winthrop, CEO and owner of Winthrop's department stores, refused to hire her students until Kiley became part of the deal. She quickly discovered that Winthrop's policy of "satisfaction guaranteed" only began to describe what Max offered....

#302 THE COWBOY Jayne Ann Krentz (Ladies and Legends, Book 3)

Sexy cowboys in pin-striped suits were writer Margaret Lark's idea of romantic heroes. Rafe Cassidy seemed to fit the picture, but he had seriously compromised his credibility once before. He'd ordered Margaret out of his life for being loyal to her boss rather than to her lover. Now he was determined to get her back—to prove his honor was safe.

#303 ONLY YESTERDAY Karen Toller Whittenburg

Merry McLennan, former "little" Miss Sunshine and child model, thought she had buried her old identity for good. She never wanted to be used again for her looks or put on display. Until she met Lee Zurbaron, a psychologist whose latest research project dealt with child stars. Once again Merry found herself in the spotlight... just where she didn't want to be.

#304 REMEMBRANCE Lynn Michaels EDITOR'S CHOICE

When Cathy Martin returned to her grandmother's home in Martha's Vineyard to coauthor the actress's memoirs, she hadn't expected to meet her grandfather's ghost. Was *he* haunting the house—or was it Fin McGraw, his look-alike? Fin was definitely flesh and blood—and eager to help Cathy explore all the bumps and noises that happen in the night....

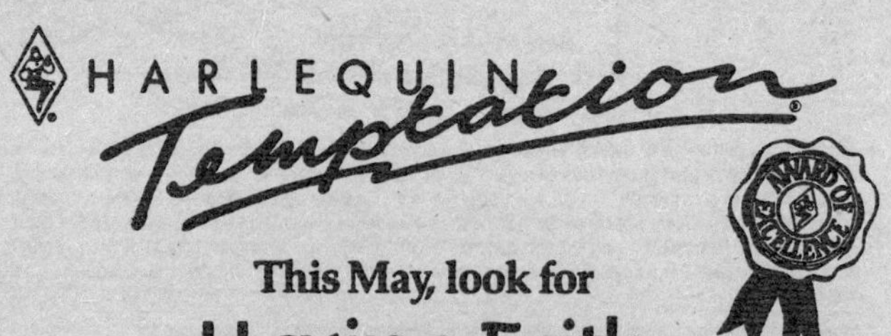
HARLEQUIN
Temptation

HARLEQUIN'S "BIG WIN" SWEEPSTAKES RULES & REGULATIONS

NO PURCHASE NECESSARY TO ENTER OR RECEIVE A PRIZE

1. To enter and join the Reader Service, scratch off the metallic strips on all your BIG WIN tickets #1-#6. This will reveal the values for each sweepstakes entry number, the number of free book(s) you will receive, and your free bonus gift as part of our Reader Service. If you do not wish to take advantage of our Reader Service, but wish to enter the Sweepstakes only, scratch off the metallic strips on your BIG WIN tickets #1-#4. Return your entire sheet of tickets intact. Incomplete and/or inaccurate entries are ineligible for that section or sections of prizes. Not responsible for mutilated or unreadable entries or inadvertent printing errors. Mechanically reproduced entries are null and void.

2. Whether you take advantage of this offer or not, your Sweepstakes numbers will be compared against a list of winning numbers generated at random by the computer. In the event that all prizes are not claimed by March 31, 1992, a random drawing will be held from all qualified entries received from March 30, 1990 to March 31, 1992, to award all unclaimed prizes. All cash prizes (Grand to Sixth), will be mailed to the winners and are payable by cheque in U.S. funds. Seventh prize to be shipped to winners via third-class mail. These prizes are in addition to any free, surprise or mystery gifts that might be offered. Versions of this sweepstakes with different prizes of approximate equal value may appear in other mailings or at retail outlets by Torstar Corp. and its affiliates.

3. The following prizes are awarded in this sweepstakes: ★ Grand Prize (1) $1,000,000; First Prize (1) $25,000; Second Prize (1) $10,000; Third Prize (5) $5,000; Fourth Prize (10) $1,000; Fifth Prize (100) $250; Sixth Prize (2500) $10; ★ ★ Seventh Prize (6000) $12.95 ARV.

   ★ This Sweepstakes contains a Grand Prize offering of $1,000,000 annuity. Winner will receive $33,333.33 a year for 30 years without interest totalling $1,000,000.

   ★ ★ Seventh Prize: A fully illustrated hardcover book published by Torstar Corp. Approximate value of the book is $12.95.

   Entrants may cancel the Reader Service at any time without cost or obligation to buy (see details in center insert card).

4. This promotion is being conducted under the supervision of Marden-Kane, Inc., an independent judging organization. By entering this Sweepstakes, each entrant accepts and agrees to be bound by these rules and the decisions of the judges, which shall be final and binding. Odds of winning in the random drawing are dependent upon the total number of entries received. Taxes, if any, are the sole responsibility of the winners. Prizes are nontransferable. All entries must be received by no later than 12:00 NOON, on March 31, 1992. The drawing for all unclaimed sweepstakes prizes will take place May 30, 1992, at 12:00 NOON, at the offices of Marden-Kane, Inc., Lake Success, New York.

5. This offer is open to residents of the U.S., the United Kingdom, France and Canada, 18 years or older except employees and their immediate family members of Torstar Corp., its affiliates, subsidiaries, Marden-Kane, Inc., and all other agencies and persons connected with conducting this Sweepstakes. All Federal, State and local laws apply. Void wherever prohibited or restricted by law. Any litigation respecting the conduct and awarding of a prize in this publicity contest may be submitted to the Régie des loteries et courses du Québec.

6. Winners will be notified by mail and may be required to execute an affidavit of eligibility and release which must be returned within 14 days after notification or, an alternative winner will be selected. Canadian winners will be required to correctly answer an arithmetical skill-testing question administered by mail which must be returned within a limited time. Winners consent to the use of their names, photographs and/or likenesses for advertising and publicity in conjunction with this and similar promotions without additional compensation.

7. For a list of our major winners, send a stamped, self-addressed envelope to: WINNERS LIST c/o MARDEN-KANE, INC., P.O. BOX 701, SAYREVILLE, NJ 08871. Winners Lists will be fulfilled after the May 30, 1992 drawing date.

If Sweepstakes entry form is missing, please print your name and address on a 3" × 5" piece of plain paper and send to:

In the U.S.
Harlequin's "BIG WIN" Sweepstakes
901 Fuhrmann Blvd.
P.O. Box 1867
Buffalo, NY 14269-1867

In Canada
Harlequin's "BIG WIN" Sweepstakes
P.O. Box 609
Fort Erie, Ontario
L2A 5X3

LTY-H590